Gay City: Volume 4

At Second Glance

First Edition

GAY CITY HEALTH PROJECT
511 E. Pike Street
Seattle, WA 98122
www.GayCity.org

Many of these selections are works of fiction. Names, characters, places and incidents depicted are either products of the contributors' imaginations or are used fictitiously. Any resemblance to actual persons, living or dead, events or locales is entirely coincidental.

ISBN-10   1466458291
EAN-13   978-1466458291

Cover design by Garth Meske
Book design by Vincent Kovar

Printed in the United States of America

Gay City: Volume 4

At Second Glance

To the friends who became family
And the family that became friends

For Alan, Ervene, and Gary:
'Thank you',
Eric

To everyone who believed.
Vincent

Published through the kind support of:

CULTURE
KING COUNTY PERCENT FOR ART

We'd also like to thank our Patrons:

Daniel Nye

Cantor David Serkin-Poole
&
Temple B'nai Torah, Bellevue

and our supporters:

Jonathan L. Bowman

Sandra Perkins

Thank You!

Contents

Inside *At Second Glance*.. 9

Frog in a Well.. 12

Edom the Treasure Keeper...29

Betrayed With a Kiss.. 40

How Should I Presume.. 55

The Not So Odd Couple..62

Benvolio: A Play in Development..70

Dickie Derringer: The Doctor is In..76

Pirate Games... 84

My Craft... 95

Harry and the Forgotten Fuckbuddy..99

Love Potion Number Nine.. 110

The End of an Era.. 115

Masquerade... 129

The Shining One... 136

A Charming Menage... 154

About Gay City.. 174

Epilogue... 179

Inside *At Second Glance*

Eric Andrews-Katz

Growing up Queer (gay/lesbian/bisexual/transgendered…anything apart from 'normal' society) gives a person the chance to look at the world with a different set of eyes. A Queer child quickly learns to identify not necessarily with what is written down in front of them, but with what is found between the lines of published literature. Or at least what is imagined to be there.

Take for example the Oscar Wilde classic The Picture of Dorian Gray. It can be a horror story, with an implied morality of the evils of vanity when read by one set of eyes, as the general public in its Victorian premier of 1890 viewed it. But when a Queer child reads the dark tale, they may come to understand the implications on a completely different level. The subtleties of homosexual undertones are more readily identifiable to those open to recognizing them. Wilde was a pioneer who purposely placed clues, like a scavenger hunt for the Queer secret society, to find, follow, and enjoy on a juxtaposed level to their non-Queer counterparts.

Even among the greatest of writers few have Wilde's genius and wit to be as blatant as he was in his day. Millions of other stories have been written, shared and enjoyed that left the readers searching for clues of a tale not told. How many Queer readers have wondered about the unexpressed friendship of Sherlock Holmes and Dr. Watson, the non-dramatized relationship between Professor Higgins and Colonel Pickering, or the sheer feminist independence of Jane Austin's Emma?

Often, we'll read and reread a particular tale wondering what might have been meant by the author's specific word choice or phrase. We'll wonder if this is another subtle clue on the literary scavenger hunt left to those of a counter-culture to find. Whether the author meant them to be there, or if they are imagined for wanting by the reader is irrelevant: we Queers have already started to, subconsciously at least, rewrite the stories we read so that we may identify with them. It is for this reason that *At Second Glance* has been put together.

Collected within these pages are stories we have already known; or at least scenarios with which we are already familiar. The difference here is that we Queers don't have to search for the hidden meanings. There is no wondering if these characters may or may not share our desires and longings. Clearly they do!

The collected stories are selected to represent a wide range of storytelling. Or in this case, retelling. Many might even be considered re-envisioned. Some are based on fairy tales that we are told from our births. But maybe as the reader follows along, they will identify in a different way with the characters found in Edom, the Treasure Keeper, Frog in a Well, or A Charming Menage. Maybe it was when reading the classic tales of literature that someone began to question what 'really was going on' in certain stories. If so, then you may identify more with Benvolio, The Not So Odd Couple, Pirate Games, or even Harry & The Forgotten Fuckbuddy. Or if you've ever wondered about the possibilities of alternative historical personalities, you may enjoy the revelations disclosed in The Shining One or Betrayed with a Kiss.

The authors represented are as various as the stories they have re-envisioned. First of all both genders have written for this anthology to further expand the viewpoints of these retold tales. Some of the authors are established and acclaimed with a list of publishing credits to their names. Others are making their anthology debut. While authors from both coasts are represented, as well as states between, a strong percentage represents local authors in regards to Gay City's physical location in Seattle.

Several major traits bind these authors together. Their obvious talent should come through first. The fact that they were all brave enough to re-envision these tales makes them pioneers in their own fashion, as much as their predecessors. But the primary factor is that they have written stories where Queers have their place with familiar characters and recognizable surroundings. For a change, we Queers are not the ones getting the literary whiplash, doing a double take to reread what is printed on the page. We don't have to search for, wonder about, and speculate within the written content between these covers. These authors have already re-envisioned them for us. The only thing left for us to do is to sit back and enjoy them.

Eric Andrews-Katz
Seattle, 2011

Frog in a Well

Ryan Keawekane

At the end of the Ming dynasty, there lived a modest couple. Newly married, Wang and his wife Yin didn't meddle in the affairs of the emperor's throne, but frogs rarely care about the affairs of humans. This couple lived in a quaint well, where they eagerly awaited their first brood. Though they were happy for the most part, all was not well in the well. Wang was rife with confusion and dissatisfaction. He was having increasingly disturbing dreams about an event that had happened recently.

One day, Wang was just sitting on a mossy stone, watching as the sunlight dappled the well waters and cast images of dancing light on the opposite wall. Suddenly, it was like night had come prematurely. Looking up, Wang saw a shadow with the vague shape of a strange bird, wings spread wide. But this bird wasn't moving. It was lingering between the well and the disk of sky, just hovering. The shadow was there and gone, followed by a little splash. Wang went over to investigate and found a small button of white jade. He had never seen anything so beautiful in his life. The surface of the button was unnaturally smooth, and it had four holes at its center, all perfectly round. Moments later, still in a reverie, Wang found a strand of hair resting on the surface of the water. It was about as long as he was squat. He picked it up, astounded by its delicacy. Thrilled with his discoveries, he thought that together they would look great around his neck. He ran the thread of hair through one of the holes in the button, then with slippery fingers managed to tie a sturdy square knot in the hair. From then on, he wore the makeshift necklace wherever he went, like a prize.

Yin must have been snoozing in one of the forty-three crevices they could reach: she missed the whole event. When she woke up, she found her husband with the button hanging around his neck. "That's very pretty," she said.

"Isn't it?" Wang said with a glimmer in his eye.

"What is it?" Yin asked.

"This is a white jade. It's very valuable... And this is a strand of human hair," he said indicating the strand around his neck.

"What's a human?"

Wang's eyes filled with wonder as he described pure nonsense to her. "Well, they are just the most beautiful creature. They have dry skin, none of this slimy stuff that you and I have. They don't jump about like us, either: they walk on only two legs. And they can only have one offspring at a time!"

"Impossible!" Yin cried. "Where do you come up with these bizarre ideas?"

"Humans are real," Wang maintained, "and the best thing about them is this grand head of hair! All long and flowy. Imagine this thing around my neck, but thousands of them, millions of them, coming out of your head!"

"Ew, gross!"

"It's pure magic!"

Yin didn't know what magic was, but she thought she wouldn't like it either. She didn't ask about what white jade might be, for fear of the answer.

It wasn't long after Wang began wearing the button necklace that he started having dreams about the shadowy head of billowing hair. Far from troubling, they were soothing and even filled him with a kind of nostalgia, a longing for something forgotten or lost. The dreams had the same quality as memories. He "remembered" humans, the women beautifully dressed in silk robes in reds and violets, upon their heads the most intricate head ornaments from either side of which beaded cascades fell, framing their pale faces. The men wore robes of blue, white, or brown, the color of which garment seeming to dictate how they treated each other. They too wore headgear of a sort: black hats with wings flaring out over the ears. The mood of these dreams was festive. Wine flowed, and an orchestra played in the background. Wang reveled in how it felt to be around them, especially since he did not look at them from below as would a frog, but walked among them, head high, chest out.

The dreams were astoundingly consistent, each one building upon the former. In an early dream, Wang was arriving at this perpetual party, greeting the men and women with a nod of the head. All bowed low to him. Wang repaired to a much smaller, though no less regal, private dining room where his personal retinue stood from their chairs to greet him with a low bow. The dreaming Wang could not help feeling like some kind of royalty.

In a later dream, Wang passed a mirror so intricately wrought that it caught his attention. But looking into the glass itself, Wang found a stunning countenance: his own. His dream self was a fine specimen of a human male. Gone were the bulbous eyes of a frog, in their place almond-shaped wonders set in a flat, pale face on either side of a long, narrow nose. His fat frog lips were now humanly thin and pink, one more delicate than the other. His attention was immediately seized by the jet-black hair just visible beneath the ceremonial hat on his head, the black wings fanning out on either side of his handsome face. His robes were of the finest material, a deep, imperial red that stirred in him feelings of pride and duty. He stood there watching the flicker of his own eyes and the pulse in his fine neck. When he reached up to touch that pulse with his fingers, he was amazed by the delicacy of his own hands, the fingertips long and tapered. At his throat, he saw a gleaming button keeping his collar in place.

Suddenly, Wang's wasn't the only handsome face in the looking glass. Wang saw a gentleman of discrimination. The slender waist flared out on top into broad shoulders, shot down below into long legs. His apparel hinted at an elevated personage, but the green of his robes set him apart from the men and women around him. Wang had never seen such a beautiful man. Now, he had seen two. Their features, he noted then, were quite similar: the same deep-brown almond eyes, long narrow nose, kissable lips--and the hint of hair peeking out from under the ceremonial hat. Wang had to meet him. But when he turned to find him, the gentleman was gone. Within moments, the dream, too, dissipated and Wang awoke in a thin film of his own goop.

"This cannot be who I really am," he whispered in the dark, interminable well. The moon, clinging to the disk of sky, seemed far away. Try though he might, Wang could not wrestle himself back to sleep and he spent the night envisioning and re-envisioning both his own dream self and the other beauty he had seen.

The gestation of their eggs kept time for the married couple. For Yin, it was business as usual, but Wang would infrequently break the silence of the well with a silly question that put the soon-to-be-mother ill at ease. On one occasion, Wang asked, "What would you think if I had a full head of hair?"

"I can't imagine anything more disgusting," Yin said honestly.

"Your problem is that you can't think bigger than this well."

"That's where you're wrong," Yin said. "Take the sky, for example. I think we are so lucky that it sits above our very own well. It could go anywhere it wanted, be blown away by the wind. But here it is, sitting on our little well, keeping us warm in the day and safe at night. We are so special."

"Yes," Wang agreed, none too convinced.

On another occasion, Yin was basking in the sun, moistening her skin with momentary dips while hunting a fly on the other side of the well with her eyes. It had descended all the way from above for a sip at their succulent waters. Then, when the fly had finally ceased zipping around and came to rest near Yin, Wang said, "I have dreams of being human..."

The fly was scared away, but Yin snatched the fly right out of the air, swallowing it down in a gulp. She pretended to be too distracted to hear her husband.

Soon, Wang and Yin welcomed their first brood. Yin had to admit that, for all his awkwardness, Wang was a wonder with the tads. He was solicitous to the point of exhaustion. They were too plentiful to name at first, but when those who would die were dead and the remaining were a more manageable number, Wang and Yin finally got around to naming them. Within a month of their spawning, only seven tads were left and gave no signs of dying. As the little ones flitted about just beneath the surface of the water, Wang turned to his wife and asked, "Why don't we name them after the colors of the rainbow?" They had seen a rainbow sailing between the well and the disk of the sky earlier that week.

"You mean like Red and Blue?" Yin asked.

"Red and Blue are so mundane. Why not Scarlet for a girl and Navy for a boy."

"I suppose..."

"Then perhaps--hmm, what is orange besides an orange?"

"What is an orange?"

"I've got it! Tangerine!"

Before Yin could object, Wang had named them all. They were thereafter called Scarlet, Tangerine, Ochre, Chartreuse (whom Yin simply called, "Charles" for fear that a boy with such a shiny name would turn out dull), Navy, and the terrible twins Indigo and Violet.

For a while, Wang was distracted enough by his fatherly duties that, for sheer exhaustion and joy, he simply did not dream. But when the tads were just beginning to sprout tiny feet, the dreams came back with all their prior fervor. Wang would catch glimpses of himself and his heart's desire in the mirror with the ornate frame. However, more and more his dreams were full of a woman whose beauty was exquisite. Her face was white like a dove feather. Her lips were unnaturally red, two lines of blood in a pool of milk. Her hair was an enviable onyx cascade. Despite her beauty, however, Wang felt repulsed by her. Something about her was wrong. All the same, Wang was forced to suffer her presence constantly. Every dream for what seemed an interminable period was full of her gorgeous face, brooding, cajoling, simpering. Meanwhile, Wang's every desire was to run off with his own double.

Finally, there came the dream that shook him to his core. It began much like the others: without preamble, smoothly moving from the events of recent dreams on toward new material. Wang was alone with the vapid vixen, touring a luxurious, lamp-lit pavilion, when she pronounced the words that sent him careening right back to the frayed edges of consciousness: "When will you make an empress of me?"

"Empress?" Wang thought wildly upon waking, mucus pouring from his skin. "How could my marrying her turn her into an empress?"

Wang could not recall a single dream or dream sequence that felt so real. He seemed incapable of dreaming of his real life: the well, Yin, or his polychromatic brood. All he ever dreamt about was the human world above. It was like he was leading two lives: frog by day, human by night.

Reconsidering the dream, he wondered if it was possible for his human doppelganger to be royalty, perhaps even the emperor's son, the high prince himself? For only by marrying the high prince could this wench hope to become empress. If it didn't feel so real, Wang might simply enjoy how entertaining these dreams were. But that woman's presence was so tangible, sultry and insipid at once. In comparison, his desire for the man in green robes grew into a ripe obsession. Wang had several distinct memories of cutting his sleeve at the first hint of dawn, for that personage had fallen asleep in his arms, and it was better to ruin the royal garment than disturb the perfection of the sleeping one's countenance. There wasn't an hour in the day when Wang wasn't harkening back to the moments they shared, whether eying each other in the mirror, or sharing passion in Wang's private quarters. Those dark eyes and sensuous lips haunted Wang, and the heat his countenance ignited in Wang's flesh was real enough to burn.

The morning after dreaming of the girl broaching the question of marriage, Wang decided he had to speak to his wife.

"Yin," he began carefully, "I've been having these dreams."

Yin's response was dry as salt and as cutting: "Of being human, right?" Wang nodded his head and she sighed a long sigh. "Forget about it, Wang, for our tads. For yourself..." Then, taking his slippery hands into hers, she added, a supplication in her voice, "For me..."

Once again Wang pushed his dreams to the back of his mind in order to focus on living the life he led and loving his wife and tads, who were growing bigger all the time. His efforts were rewarded with several weeks of blissful parenthood, during which he said nothing about the dreams that continued to haunt him. He might have lived the rest of his life that way, if it weren't for the rat that literally fell into his lap.

Wang had been floating in the water, dozing on his back, when the rat fell from the sky. It knocked the wind right out of him, the weight of the rat's huge body dragging him down to the bottom of the well. The splash caught everyone's attention. Yin, Scarlet, and Charles were quickest to act, diving down to save Wang. They laid him out on a bed of moss and resuscitated him, while the rest of the tads went to save the rat, which would surely drown otherwise. A dead rat was a stink rat. They were fortunate to live in a shallow well, Yin thought as her tads managed to prop the rat with his head above water.

Meanwhile, Wang had coughed up all the water he'd swallowed and was resting on his side. His children drew a rainbow of worry around him as his breathing returned to normal. He was shaken but fine. The rat, a male named Shu, was also fine, though he appeared to have sprained his leg. He had been caught "relieving the humans of their surplus, when some little whip threw me in here!"

"Humans?" Wang asked, perking up.

"What is surplus?" Yin wanted to know.

"Excess food and stuff," Wang hurriedly answered.

"This guy knows his stuff," Shu said. Then, he added, "This isn't the first time I was caught, though it is the first time they threw me down a well. With all that food and all that 'majesty,' you'd think they'd let an honest rat take care of his family. Now, this... Looks like I'll have to rely on the largess of your family for the next little while."

"It's no problem," Wang said. Then, noting the rat's diction, he added, "No offense, but you're quite well educated for a rat."

"I could say something similar about you," the rat replied.

"I just try to keep abreast of things... Nothing fancy."

Shu's eyebrows rose at that. "'Fancy' is all the palace is about. That and scandal, ever since the emperor's nephew was named crown prince a couple years ago..."

Wang was stunned by that. "Why wouldn't the emperor pass the throne down to his own son?"

"The emperor is dead, and the High Prince Zhen disappeared."

Yin lost interest in all this talk of humans and hopped away, but Wang was intent on learning more. According to the rat, Prince Zhen had been wooing a certain Duchess Xia. Xia was the deceased emperor's niece, sister of the very nephew that had recently been named crown prince, Duke Lu. By all accounts, the prince and his consort were on the eve of announcing their betrothal when Prince Zhen suddenly disappeared. Moments before his disappearance, in the midst of a grand dinner party, Prince Zhen was seen exchanging heated words with Xia when her brother the duke found them. Several informants claimed that Prince Zhen and Duchess Xia ran off together, leaving Duke Lu to tend to the guests until his sister the duchess returned, which she did around midnight when she gave every indication that there would be no announcement of the nuptial sort that night--or ever.

But there was another version of the story, which piqued Wang's interest. Shu said, "Some say it's true that the Prince didn't leave with the duchess: he left with someone else, a man called the Honorable Hao. The two were a lot alike, in countenance, refinement, and manner, enough to pass for brothers. They were, in fact, best friends. Some say too good of friends, if you know what I mean..."

"I don't..." Wang said breathlessly.

"Well, according to this story, Prince Zhen and Duchess Xia were fighting because Prince Zhen had decided not to marry her. He wouldn't marry anyone--at least not yet. Duchess Xia was right to be furious; without the marriage, she would never rise above her rank. Her brother the duke was also furious when plans for the nuptials were dashed, and for much the same reason. As it turns out, Prince Zhen's disappearance was much more fortuitous for Duke Lu, though the duchess' status will be little improved when her brother becomes the Son of Heaven."

"Duke Lu cannot become emperor!" Wang shouted.

But, Shu informed Wang, it made perfect sense. Prince Lu had built a concrete alliance with Prince Zhen's cabinet and military division. So much so that, when the prince disappeared, his cabinet took less than a week to name Lu crown prince, a decision they assured the populace that their honorable ancestors and the deceased emperor himself would have sanctioned. Lu relocated his stronghold to the palace, bringing his hateful wife with him.

"Duchess Boli..." Wang whispered.

"That's her," Shu agreed. "Wow, you really do get the news down here!"

Duchess Boli was as much a blight on the palace and its hands as the now Crown Prince Lu was on his kingdom and its lands. While her husband went out looking for lands to conquer, she stayed at home where Duchess Boli did some conquering of her own. She indulged in her every whim precisely because no one could tell her otherwise. The humans weren't the only ones suffering under their reign of terror. The animals of the palace had even more reason to fear, for on any given day their lives might be forfeit to the duchess and her uneven temperament.

"I was lucky," the rat said solemnly. "The boy who caught me didn't know what to do with me. Most other rats are killed and fed to the dogs, and not necessarily in that order."

"Has no one heard from Prince Zhen?" Wang wondered aloud.

Shu shook his head. "No, but we all wish he'd come back. Even if he 'cut his sleeve' for the Honorable Hao, no one cares at this point."

Wang was surprised to hear reference to his dream, but didn't say anything to the rat. Instead, he said, "Whatever happened to this man, Prince Zhen's... consort?"

"He is still in the court, though primarily so the Duchesses Xia and Boli can torture him. Besides, they want to keep Hao around as leverage, in case the prince returns."

"What kind of leverage could they possibly use him for?" Wang asked.

"Well, according to my informant--"

"Oh, who are you kidding?" Wang said in exasperation.

"Oh, all right, it's me," the rat admitted. "So one time, I heard Xia tell Boli that she caught Prince Zhen alone with his 'consort.' Let's say they were in a very compromising position. Prince Zhen and Hao were shaken that Xia caught them. I bet that was what forced the Prince's hand. If he wanted Xia to keep quiet about it, Prince Zhen would have to marry her."

"I see," Wang said feeling sick to his stomach. He took his leave of the rat shortly thereafter. He expected the dreams to come that night, and he was not disappointed. After days and weeks of waiting, he knew he would finally see more of that handsome young man, whom he now knew was called the Honorable Hao.

Wang and Hao were in a small service corridor between two enormous bedroom chambers. Unlike the rooms where the imperials walked and talked, ate and drank, this corridor was bare, the walls a dull ruddy brown reminiscent of dried blood. The only furniture was a small square table, beside it a single chair. Hao was sitting in the chair, looking straight at the wall before him, his brow furrowed. Wang was kneeling beside him, eyes on the young beauty.

"Hao," Wang in Prince Zhen's skin said, "we can't go on like this."

"I know, my prince, but what can we do?"

"We can run."

"Run?" Hao said, looking up in disbelief. "How can you run away from your own kingdom, my prince?"

"None of it means anything, if I can't be with you, Hao."

"You know I can't let you do that. I love you, but--"

"You love me?" Wang asked, shocked to hear Hao speak those three words.

20

"Well, of course, I love you; you're my prince and one day soon you'll be my king."

"But that's not what you meant!" Wang said, a little too vehemently.

"Keep your voice down. People may hear us."

"So let them! I'm sick of hiding. I'm not ashamed of my feelings for you. Are you?"

Hao looked up at the prince, eyes moist. Then, Hao shook his head. "No... I think I have loved you since the day I was born."

"Then let me be your king and your king alone," Wang said. "Run away with me..."

They sat there for a moment in that tiny service corridor, Wang kneeling beside the man he loved. Neither could take his eyes from the other. Finally, Hao nodded, weakly at first, then with increasing certainty. "I could have never lived this lie. If I allowed you to cut your sleeve even once more, the cabinet might have grounds to believe that you would forsake your duty as emperor to father an heir to the throne... You're right: we have to run away."

Swept up by such tremendous emotion, Wang wrapped his arms around Hao, his childhood friend and confidante, now the man of his dreams and--with luck--his future. At first, the embrace was like many they had shared, each with his head on the other's shoulder. But as they held each other closer, their faces hovering perilously close, their cheeks touched. Eyes closed, Wang searched for his friend's lips with his own. Wang found Hao's delicate mouth open, waiting, inviting, and they kissed for the first time, and for ever. Eyes closed they could not see the door open, though they heard the door close with a loud report and then the sound of someone running off. Wang knew it had to be Duchess Xia.

Guilt and shame were their first reactions, but Wang assured Hao that this didn't change their plans at all. "We run away tonight," he said.

However, when next Wang saw the duchess, he knew she had him cornered. With a few coy moves, Xia had forced him into agreeing to a marriage of convenience. Wang went from a free man full of love to a prisoner full of shame. How would he tell Hao? Wang could not bring himself to confide in his one and only confidante. Through his tumultuous childhood as a spoiled child, and with the death of his father the emperor, Prince Zhen had suffered all manner of misfortunes. But until that day he had never hated his lot as high prince more. Meanwhile,

Duchess Xia made immediate arrangements for the dinner party where their engagement would be announced.

"Yin," Wang said to his wife the next day, "do you remember me from before the day we met?"

"Well, I should, I mean, we lived in the same well for our entire lives!" She laughed dryly.

"Did we?"

"Of course, we did!" Yin cried, forcefully, a strange expression on her face.

"You mean I didn't fall from the sky, like Shu?"

"What? How would that be--? Did that rat--? Why, I ought to--"

"Just answer the question, Yin. Did I fall from the sky, like Shu?"

Yin began to fret. Her whole life was crumbling down around her. She didn't know what to say. So she said nothing, but it was enough for Wang. He slipped off into the water and headed for the other side of the well where Shu the rat was still recuperating.

"Where are you going?" she asked.

"Back," was all Wang said.

"Back where?"

"Back where I came from!"

"But what about your tads? What about me?" Yin was a blubbering mess of tears. Her voice and the distress in it had roused their brood, which began to gather around her, every hue of concern.

"They're yours now! That's all you ever wanted, anyway: not to be alone."

"But how can you leave your home?" she cried. "This well is everything to us! We have the water around us, not too deep, not too shallow! We have the mud and the moss, to massage our tired feet. We are the king and queen of our little domain. Even the sky above is for us alone!"

From the other side of the well, Wang cried back, "You think the sky is just a silly disk that sits on top our little well--like a lid? It isn't a disk: it spans from one side of the world to the other, but you can't even imagine that, can you? And this water--there is an ocean out there, thousands and thousands of miles wide, and unknown fathoms deep! How do I know? I've seen it with my own eyes. My human eyes. If you love this well so much, you stay in it. I'm getting out of here."

Shu the rat had been watching the whole charade, but he took his cue now as Wang hopped up to him. "So it really is you, High Prince Zhen?"

"I believe it is," said Wang, awkwardly.

"I suspected it the minute I met you."

"Why?" Wang asked.

"Who else would name himself 'king'?" Wang laughed, because that was indeed his name. "Do you think you can get us back out on dry land?"

"I think so," Shu said, testing his leg. "Thanks to you and your family, my leg is much better. But first answer me one question: how did you end up a frog?"

"I don't know," Wang said, "but I think I know someone who does."

Wang climbed on Shu's back and slowly, they climbed back out to the surface. Night had fallen. Wang told Shu to take him to Duchess Xia's bedchambers. The duchess would be preparing for bed soon, but first Wei, the chambermaid, would have to freshen up the duchess' quarters. Wei was an unassuming girl who had always made herself available to Wang's every wish, so he liked her. Besides, if anyone in the palace knew anything about magic potions, it was likely to be Wei, who came from a long line of witches who weren't above using magic to get things done. With Wang on his back, Shu slithered through the interconnected network of tunnels, runoffs, and vents woven through the palace like threads in a tapestry. They found Wei as expected, straightening up Duchess Xia's room. Wang was happy to see her, but distraught to find her underfed with sallow skin and hollow cheeks.

He called to her from a vent above, "Wei!" With one great hop, he landed on the bed.

"Who's there?"

"It's me, Prince Zhen!" Wang said.

"Oh, dear!" Wei fretted. "I'm hearing voices!"

"I'm here on the bed!"

Wei looked on the bed and saw Wang the frog. "Ew, pesky little vermin! Get off the duchess' bed!" She swatted at him with her hand.

"I am not a 'pesky little vermin'!" Wang cried. "I am your prince and you will obey my orders."

"Prince Zhen?" Wei said, her eyes wide. "Oh, no... Am I in trouble?"

"Not if you can tell me how to get out of this," Wang said.

Wei admitted that she had provided Duchess Xia with the concoction that transformed Prince Zhen into a frog. "She slipped it in your wine, my prince. If I knew what she was going to do, I wouldn't have let her, but we country folk aren't too bright..."

"It's all right, Wei. Just tell me how to reverse the spell."

It was simple: all he needed was for a princess to kiss him. Then, he would be transformed back into human form.

"Perfect!" Wang said without a trace of hope. "There hasn't been a princess in this kingdom since before my father died." Wang slumped down on the bed. But he was spurred to reserve a little hope, if not for himself, then for someone else. "What about... the Honorable Hao?" he asked, tentatively.

"The errand boy?" Wei asked.

"They've made an errand boy of an aristocrat?!" Wang cried, his heart broken.

"Is it true what they say, then?" Wei asked.

"Tread lightly," Shu the rat advised the girl, but too late.

"What who says?" Wang asked.

"Well, people have been talking, my prince, saying you had cut your sleeve for him..."

Wang had heard enough. He could have pretended that the rumors weren't true. But he hadn't crawled out of one dark hole to crawl back into another. "Yes," he said with finality. "It's all true. I love the Honorable Hao and have since the day I first laid eyes on him. And if he hasn't completely lost faith in me, I will do everything in my power to prove my love to him."

Wei nodded and smiled. Then, a thought occurred to her. "But, my prince, what about your kingdom?"

"Who says I can't have both?"

Suddenly, there came the sound of Duchess Xia's voice in the corridor outside. Those in her bedchambers scattered. Wang leapt off the bed and hid underneath it, while Shu scampered off and Wei hurriedly finished preparing the duchess' effects. From his perch, Wang watched the door open and heard Duchess Xia order Wei out and close the door. Xia doused the candles that Wei had only just lit and clambered into bed.

Wang smelled wine and knew the duchess was drunk. As the bed creaked under Xia's weight, Wang's brain began to work. He thought he might have a plan. He waited for a while, before coming out from under the bed. He jumped onto the bed and sidled toward the duchess' head, guided by the stench of alcohol on her breath. He climbed up beside her ear, then whispered in the silkiest voice, "Duchess Xia, it is me, your prince. I'm here to marry you. All you have to do is kiss me, and the kingdom is yours..."

"Prince Zhen?" Xia said groggily.

"Shhh, my pet, no need to wake. But let us marry tonight, right now, my love! Kiss me, Duchess Xia, and become my empress!"

Slowly, Xia turned toward Wang's voice and, with all the fervor of one entangled in the snares of an elicit dream, Duchess Xia kissed Wang the frog. A grand racket followed immediately, rousing the duchess out of her bed with a scream, which called the chambermaid Wei to action. Open swung the door and in came Wei, brandishing a candelabra full of light. Even Shu the rat, who had gone off to rustle some grub, came back at the sound of the commotion. All eyes fell on the source of the surprise: a beautifully naked Prince Zhen sitting on the floor beside the duchess' bed.

"Prince Zhen?" Xia cried.

"The one and only," the prince said.

"That's impossible! You're--"

"A frog?" he asked. "Yes, well, I was one until you most generously kissed me..."

Wei lit up then, saying, "A princess!"

From up above them, Shu the rat chimed in, saying, "The duchess is a princess?"

"I am not a princess!" Xia said impetuously, stomping her bare foot. "You can't be human, because you need a princess to kiss you."

"In the strictest terms, Xia, you are a princess," Prince Zhen said. "You see, when I suddenly disappeared, my cabinet needed to find someone with enough quality and distinction to fill in during my absence. Naturally they couldn't find anyone, but your sneaky brother strong-armed them into naming him crown prince. In doing so, they effectively did what I did not: they made you a princess."

"And all he needed was one kiss!" Wei finished for him. "And poof, he's back in business!"

"Yes, I am," the Prince said. "That means that you, Duchess Xia, are no longer a princess."

"No!" Xia cried.

"What's going on?" said a familiar voice from the hallway. Hao, the honorable aristocrat turned humble errand boy, appeared in the doorway then. An errant glare from the candle blinded him and for a moment he could have sworn that his lover the prince had returned in the flesh. But when he looked again, he saw that he was not mistaken. Prince Zhen had returned. Hao could not keep tears from overflowing onto his cheeks. "My prince..."

"Hao," Prince Zhen said as he took his beloved into his arms, for nothing could keep them apart.

Xia flew into a righteous rage, throwing herself bodily first at Hao, then at the prince. "I'll kill you! I'll kill you both!"

Together, Prince Zhen and Hao stayed her hands. "Attacking your sovereign is punishable by death," Prince Zhen said. "But do me a service and I will let you live your pitiful, odious life."

"Why should I believe that you'll do anything other than have me killed as a lesson?" she cried.

"I suppose I could do that, but you haven't even heard my offer. You may like it, or have you given up all pretenses to the crown?"

"What?" Hao and Xia said together.

"It is a simple plan, but genius. When I become the Son of Heaven, I will need an heir, and the people will need an empress. I, however, have no need of an empress, but every need of you, Hao. So I will give Xia her beloved throne, but to you, Hao, I give my heart and soul."

"Zhen," Hao said softly. "How can we...?"

"We can, because I have dreamed of seeing you again, and here you are. We can, because I was once a petty prince and also a lowly creature, but now I am whole again, and wholly grateful. Finally, we can, because I will be emperor, and you will be my Distinguished Vizier. I shall have no need to ever cut my sleeves again."

So it was settled. Before the prince had had enough time to don his majestic robes and his ceremonial hat, the palace was roused from its slumber with chants of "Prince Zhen is returned! Long live the Son of Heaven! Long live Vizier Hao!" Duke Lu and Duchess Boli were ousted from the palace and returned to their piddly town as commoners, another

26

family of honest nobility supplanting them in the seat of power. Everyone recalled their vileness as rulers and, for the rest of their days, they enjoyed nothing--not food nor water, clothing nor shelter--that they themselves didn't prepare, for no one would help them.

Later that night, in the privacy of Prince Zhen's bedchambers, Hao said, "After you left, I didn't leave my chambers for days. Even after I left my room, I wouldn't go far. I favored this quiet area not far from the palace grounds where there is a common well. I would look down into the well and wish that I could hide away in it. I thought, 'Those frogs have no idea how lucky they are.' I lost my jade button in that well..."

Hearing this, Prince Zhen remembered the necklace of hair with the white jade button that had started it all: the dreams, the longing, even his romance and family life with Yin. When he had turned back into a human, the strand of hair was broken, but he had stooped to pick up the tiny jade button before it could be lost forever. Now, he took it out from a pouch he always kept near and pressed it into Hao's open hand. He said, "This frog knows how lucky he was and how lucky he is..."

Yin the frog lived in a well surrounded by her colorful children, but she was not very happy, for her tads' brood would soon take over the whole of the little well. There simply wasn't enough room in the well for all of them, but there wasn't a way for any of them to get out either. When the eggs had started to hatch and Yin had begun to think that the future could be no darker, it darkened exceptionally. The source of that darkness turned out to be a shadow--of a head. A human head framed by a funny hat with wings that looked like a bird from inside the well.

"Yin!" a voice boomed "Are you there?"

"Who is it?" Yin called back.

"It's me, Wang--though I am called Prince Zhen up here!"

"Wang!" Yin cried in a mixture of joy and guilt. "Have you come back to your well?"

"I have, but I cannot stay, and I don't think you should, either."

"What do you mean?" Yin asked. Her children were listening intently, too.

"As I said, there is a great ocean with water as far as the eye can see, stretching for thousands and thousands of miles. I can take you all to it, so everyone can have a brighter future..."

"The ocean is too big!" Yin objected. "I might drown! What would anyone need so much water for?"

"Our children are having children of their own, and you and I both know that you can't all survive down there in such cramped quarters. Our children and their children and their children's children will have all the room in the world to swim and play and find happiness."

"You're right," she said. "But I don't want to go. I prefer to be alone. Take our children, but leave me be. I am happy in this well. Promise only to leave me my sky, my water, and my well."

"I promise," said the Prince, and he and his vizier returned to the palace to contemplate relocating the frogs and their tads to a bigger, better, brighter place than the bottom of a silly well.

As for Shu the rat, let us say that he had no more difficulty fending for his family.

Ryan Keawekane

moved from Hilo, Hawaii, to Seattle in 2003. He quickly fell in love with William Rowden. With his encouragement, Ryan returned to school and became the first in his family to graduate from college. Ryan now uses his Linguistics degree in his work as a technical editor. When not traveling the world, Ryan and William live in Wedgwood with a spoiled black cat named Feistel and one of their best friends, Teri.

Edom the Treasure Keeper

Casondra Brewster

In the land of the giants, you were told how to live, what job you would do and what mate you could or couldn't have. The Council of Seers, in advisement to the King, decided when a giant was born what his or her life would be. Through visions and meditations, they set the life course of every giant in the kingdom, save the king himself. Although the seers within the council worked for the crown more closely than some professions, they didn't get to choose what path their lives would take either. It was the way of the giants.

When Edom was born to a farmer and baker, the oldest seer on the council had the strongest vision she had her entire long life. She said that the young giant would be the keeper of the King's treasures, most notably the Golden Harp. The Golden Harp was an entrapped fairy whose voice and musical spell-making could soothe even the angriest giant. He helped keep the King's enemies at bay. Keeping the Golden Harp safe and happy became Edom's job, which started when he was just a lad. Feige, the fairy entrapped in the harp, grew to love the red-haired boy giant. Edom would tell Feige the stories of ancient ones, who had escaped the land of the humans and now lived in these castles in the sky, leaving their diminutive cousins to the ground far below. Those tales always made the Golden Harp shiver, so Edom would make sure he would make the Golden Harp's prisoner, Feige, laugh with his silliness. When the harp laughed the King felt good that he still held onto this treasure, as it had been stolen from the humans during the battle for the sky land.

"Edom, oh fair giant among ogres, you make my life tolerable," Feige said, his green jewel eyes the only color on his monochromatic golden body. His spine also the spine of the harp, seemed to sparkle with more fierceness when he was pleased. Edom would thank him with another of his performances, the treasure keeper not stopping until Feige would smile.

One afternoon, when Edom was just getting his chin whiskers, the King's son, Prince Tyr, came and listened to Edom's tales of the ancients. The stories of the great warriors and rulers of old excited young Tyr. He would stare into Edom's eyes and see the two of them side by side, battling the selfish humans, to keep the culture of the giants free.

"We would be great warriors, you and I," Prince Tyr told Edom.

Feige cried out in his sing-song voice, "No-no-nooooooo. Peace is now."

"But I was born as a warrior for all of the giants!" Prince Tyr argued. "How dare you say I have no use?" He grabbed the harp and seemed ready to toss it down out of the sky kingdom.

"Wait, Tyr, my friend," Edom said. "You can help me protect the King's most precious treasure, The Golden Harp." He slowly took the harp back from Prince Tyr, stopping to caress the prince's golden locks out of his fiery hazel eyes.

"Thank you, my dearest and bravest friend," Prince Tyr held Edom's gaze for a moment before embracing the treasure keeper. "You have given me much to consider, Edom. Thank you."

"Yes," Feige said. "Between Edom's mastery of words and your swordsmanship; all will be well."

Prince Tyr was pleased with that and told his father, the King. Within days, Edom was given a small stone house on the King's Castle's grounds. There was a giving ceremony where almost all the giants in the kingdom were present. They watched as King Alf and Prince Tyr gave the keys to Edom and had The Golden Harp sing his praises. Along with The Golden Harp, there were a few other treasures Edom was given to keep close to him in the stone house. Prince Tyr gave Edom a new battle axe with which to keep any thieves away from the treasure. Included in Edom's responsibility to the King and Prince was a hen that laid golden eggs and a silver platter and goblet that filled with bread and wine on command. Again, both treasures were spoils of war from the battle with the humans. However, storytellers kept the legend going that the platter and goblet were originally from the giants' deep forestlands of old. Edom had heard those stories, he had shared them with Feige many times, practicing for the moments when he was called upon to go beyond his treasure-keeper duties and entertain the King and his guests.

One day when Edom and Prince Tyr were grown, the prince visited the treasure keeper after the fierce prince had returned from battling and uprising by humans in the far reaches of the sky kingdom.

"It is so good to see you, Edom," Prince Tyr. "How I missed our time together. Tell me a good old warrior story, please."
So Edom shared for the first time, the story of how Feige came to be with the giants.

"The Warrior King Freyr dispatched his army to the great plains of the northern human empire," Edom said in a low, yet powerful voice. "Our people had been victorious, but the soldiers were weary." Edom marched; his knees bobbing up and down in a steady rhythm that made Feige hum a battle song. Tyr bounced with slight, small movements in his seat to the four-count beat of Edom's marching.

"King Freyr wanted his fellow warriors to rest and rejuvenate themselves for the warring days to come. A giant tree was felled. Its trunk and branches made a great bonfire for the soldiers to sing and dance about. Its stump was used as a table to host the silver platter and goblet – so that all could break bread and drink their full of wine.

"Hardrada í vísdómi er dýrð," King Freyr chanted three times. A small hum came from inside the goblet and the platter shook for just a moment, the soldiers all watching with great anticipation, when loaves of bread began to fill the platter, appearing from thin air to fill the platter without end. The goblet, as well, filled to the brim with wine.

"Hundreds of giants drank their fill and ate thousands of loaves of bread that night. Sleepy with full stomachs and wine, the soldiers, as well as King Freyr slept like the tree they had felled until nearly noon. The cawing of a crow woke them. Hungry with a hangover, the soldiers looked for the platter for bread. It was gone. Stolen while the giants slept. King Freyr was enraged. Search parties were dispatched deep into the dark forest. Askr, a regimental captain, had eight soldiers with her. They penetrated the deepest parts of the woods. Just when they thought they could go no further, Askr heard a song so beautiful, it forced her and her fellow soldiers to stop and put their weapons down. For many moments they just stood there, statue-like, listening to the song and its owner's hypnotic voice."

Edom always paused at this point in the story and gave a loving look to Feige.

"A crow cawed again – Askr was shook from her trance. Her instinct was to roar a battle call. Askr's bellow did the trick and the other soldiers shuddered back into the moment. A moment that in the swiftness of a headshake was filled with a blinding light coming from the depths of the forest, like an illuminated flower head floating above the ground, which grew and multiplied like splashing raindrops. A thousand fey were upon Askr and the rest. The battle drove them deeper into the dense, overgrown woods. Askr and her fellow warriors became separated, pushed apart by the tangled arms of the underbrush. Askr dodged and fought off the fey who tried to make her bleed to death with hundreds of cuts. But the wine the night before had made her blood thin, and she found her stamina leave her more quickly than any other battle she had endured before this fight with the forest fey. Exhausted, she fell to her knees and slammed down, face-first, into the earth. The fey regrouped and carried Askr into a clearing on the other end of the forest, where a small house and pasture dotted the landscape. The sun began to set and the fey left Askr behind the cottage. In due time, Askr awoke and heard a man yelling.

"Give me bread and wine!" Askr heard through the wooden walls and small window cut-out.

Askr rose, using her sword to gain her balance. With a deep breath, she crept around to the front of the cottage, raised her sword and charged through the door.

A small manlike creature, which wasn't even as tall as Askr's hand, crouched over the King's silver platter and goblet. His ears were huge and his nose long and pointy. Ask stuck him down with a single blow of her mighty sword."

"Wait, a woman did this?" Prince Tyr asked, his eyes intensely looking at Edom.

Edom nodded and continued the story,

"She gathered the King's treasure and began to head out back into the setting sun, when she heard the low grunting of a hen. Behind her was the most brilliant auburn and black and white hen. Her hunger got the best of her and she grabbed the hen, too, intending to roast it. When

Askr grabbed the hen, it screeched, and an egg hit the cottage floor. An egg of the purest gold. She grabbed a sack and stuck the egg and hen in it.

" 'Where do you think you're going with that, thief?' Askr heard a voice. Above on the mantle of the cottage sat a Golden Harp, its long pillar was the body of a being." Edom winked at Feige. Prince Tyr gave the harp a sideways glance.

" 'To the victor goes the spoils of battle,' Askr said.

In response, the being in the harp began to sing; no words came from him, just melody. It immediately made Askr want to put down her load and fall asleep. She did put down her load, but resisted falling asleep. She grabbed some goat's wool that was in a basket waiting to be spun, and shoved it in the being's mouth, then took a leather tie from her bracer and gagged the being. She then put the harp into the sack with the hen, tied the platter to her chest and the goblet to her belt, and headed out into the evening, hurrying to get back to the camp of King Freyr."

"The spoils of war have brought you into our life – my life," Tyr said, wearing a wounded bravado as he stood between the harp and Edom.

"That and the Council of Seers," Edom said.

"I think more is at work here, Edom," Prince Tyr shifted his weight and heavily sighed. He looked as if he might say something, but simply embraced Edom, instead. "I bid you good night; I grow weary of stories spoken and unspoken. Edom tilted his head and raised an eyebrow, perplexed, and watched the prince leave his cottage and hiked the path to the castle proper.

"He is in love with you, Edom," Feige said.

"I know Tyr is fond of me; I entertain him and keep his future riches safe."

"No," Feige said. "He feels for you like that of a lover." Edom was silent and just stared at Feige.

"It is true," Feige said.

"It cannot be," Edom said. He was quiet a moment and looked with hurtful eyes at the golden harp. "I have no time for love; the Council of Seers said I shall be a solo traveler through my life. Serving only at the King's bidding."

"He is the King's son; however, Edom," Feige said. Edom feigned boredom and lay down on his cot, "That story makes me sleepy every time. I must rest."

Feige played a wonderful melody and softly sang a lullaby for Edom, who faded into slumber quickly.

Meanwhile, Prince Tyr went to speak to his father, King Alf. "What is it, son?"

"It is difficult, what I must confess, father," Prince Tyr said.

"Tell me, you are my son."

"It is Edom, father." Prince Tyr's voice cracked and he had to silence himself before he lost control and openly wept.

"What is it about Edom?"

"Edom, he..."

"Out with it, Prince! Has he stolen the treasures?"

"No! Father! Nothing like that, well something, like that,"

"Well what is it, then?" The King was growing impatient.

"The only thing, dear Edom has stolen, father, is my heart."

"Your what?"

"My heart," Prince Tyr looked at his boots.

The King was silent, but Prince Tyr knew he did not look pleased.

Moments later King Alf sighed and said, "You are my only child; my only heir. You must continue our lineage. You must take a wife and have children."

"I could have a wife as well," Prince Tyr. "If I must bear an heir."

"Children not born in a marriage of love...You must forget this silly love," King Alf said, and then he bellowed for his manservant to bring him the Golden Harp.

Prince Tyr looked all around him. The castle was such a big place. There was so many servants and advisers moving in and out of the many rooms. Yet, he knew he was very much alone. He had just bared his soul, confessed his deepest secret to his father and his father had asked for the stupid harp?

Once the harp arrived, King Alf sent the prince away to his quarters. Prince Tyr went without argument.

"Feige, I need music to soothe my disapointed heart," King Alf said.

Feige played and sang. The King listened, but his heart was not put right, even after much music was shared.

"My lord, is there some other song you'd prefer?" Feige asked, sensing the King's ill temper.

"Feige, you know Edom well, yes?"

"I do, sire, I do."

"Does he have feelings for my son?"

"Excuse me, King Alf?"

The King looked about and leaned closer to Feige, "Does Edom love my son? Is he in-love with him?"

"Sire, I am aware that Prince Tyr has strong feelings for Edom; but Edom knows his requirement – his responsibilities – to the crown."

"Does he love the prince?"

"I do not think in the same manner as Prince Tyr, sire," Feige said and softly hummed.

"Who does Edom love?" the King asked.

"Stories, sire; he loves his stories and his service to you and Prince Tyr as treasure keeper."

"I see," King Alf said and sent the harp back to be kept with Edom.

Later that evening, King Alf summoned Prince Tyr.

"We will begin the hunt for a wife for you immediately," the king told the prince.

"So, I may have Edom live in the castle?"

"No!" bellowed King Alf.

"Father," Prince Tyr began, but his father cut off his words.

"No; you will cease this silliness at once. Edom is not in love with you."

"Lies! I know he loves me; I am the Prince," Tyr cried.

"Edom knows his role. He knows his responsibility to our people; he will not bring this kingdom to its knees."

"Then I guess, now, I know mine," Prince Tyr said.

"Good! Tomorrow we leave to search the kingdom for a bride for you!"

Prince Tyr left his father's company and found himself without forethought headed straight for Edom's cottage.
He burst in to find Edom eating a poor man's stew.

"Prince Tyr! To what do I owe this evening visit?"

"I want you to come with me; we will go and rule the human lands as our people were meant to do."

"I love my life here, Tyr; why would I go to constantly battle with mankind?"

"Because you love me and I love you; but, my father is going to take me away to find a wife. I cannot abide such a farce."

"Tyr," Edom stood. "You are my friend; but, that is where the feelings end."

"You will not come with me? You do not love me?"

"You are my friend," Edom said. "My friend."

"Have my father's advisers already gotten to you? Have they threatened you?"

Edom shook his head and looked to the Golden Harp. Feige played a soft melody in sync with Tyr's disbelief. "My life is here," Edom whispered. "I'm sorry, Tyr."

"You will be!" Tyr yelled and left. Edom didn't watch him go. He just stared down at the floor of the cottage. The night was quiet except the sound of Prince Tyr's retreating steps.

"He will return," Feige tried to soothe Edom, who had begun crying silently.

But Tyr did not return. Not the next morning or the day after that. In fact, it would be many more days before the prince was seen again.

The prince had left Edom's cottage and journeyed straight to the deep western forest that connected the human's terra and the giant's sky lands. He descended down into the dark woods and began to search for the summer queen of the fairies, the rightful owner of Feige, the Golden Harp. He searched out the ancient land where King Freyr had felled the giant fairy tree and used it as a table for the silver platter and goblet – in that ancient battle more than a century ago.

"Fey Queen, show yourself! I am Tyr, son of Alf, descendant of Freyr; and I wish to return your dear Feige."
The night noises of the forest – the insects and frogs fell silent.
Tyr cried out again, "Fey Queen, show yourself." He waited. Nothing. He sat down upon the ancient stump and began to weep.
Just when Tyr thought he might have no tears left to cry, he heard what sounded like a flock of birds descending around him.

"A giant weeping is more than I can stand," a light and airy voice said.

Tyr looked around and could see nothing at first, and then at his feet, he saw a plant begin to sprout and grow. A green stalk that raised as fast a winter's wind. Its rapid ascent forced the giant prince to stand, stumbling a bit as the earth below him slightly shook. The giant stalk soon had a giant bud that opened to reveal the largest sunflower he had ever seen. In the center of it, stood the Fey Queen.

"Prince Tyr," the light and airy voice came from the small-winged creature in the center of the humongous sunflower. "I am Lyddia, Summer Queen." She stood at the same height as the prince, given the sunflower's height. She wore a gown of white and daisies danced in her gold hair. She had radiance and Prince Tyr lost his breath for a moment just looking at her. "What seems to be the trouble?"

The prince gave a bow, "Thank you for answering my call."

"I had to," Lyddia said. "A giant crying. There must be fun to be had."

"Treasure. There is treasure to be had," Prince Tyr said.

"Do tell," Lyddia cooed.

Prince Tyr told his tale. How his father had denied him the love he wanted. He explained that if he could help her get Feige back, his father would shun Edom – send him away – and they could be together. In exile, but together.

Lyddia sat down on the sunflower and thought. As she thought, Tyr's thought turned to the remembered story of Askr and looked around him, worried he may have inadvertently given the fey an opportunity to slay a giant. But he did come offering an alliance of sorts.

"I have the perfect solution," Lyddia said. "Give me your hand."

Prince Tyr held out his hand. Lyddia dropped three seeds into it.

"What is this?" he looked at the three pale pebble-like things in his palm.

"Magic seeds," she said.

"I offer battle and you give me seeds?"

"This, my giant, lover," Lyddia breathed, "This is much more efficient, and puts our common foe, mankind, as the fodder for your father's wrath.

"How?"

"Go and find an unsuspecting soul in the human village to the south. Trade him the seeds for something of value. Bring me whatever is traded for the seeds."

"I can't as a giant just go marching into the village..." and before he had the whole sentence out, Prince Tyr's felt as if he was falling to his knees. He looked up, the stalk with Lyddia's perch was many feet above him. He touched his face and then his belly, the world around him was growing and he realized he was shrinking.

"You have 24 hours; so hurry," Lyddia said.

Prince Tyr threw his cloak over himself and dashed through the woods and entered the southern village right at dawn as the market square was coming alive. He watched to see if one of the vendors seemed more reasonable or vulnerable to take his seeds for but none revealed themselves. So he waited and watched. Eventually the half-day meal was approaching and he would need to get back to Lyddia. He started asking each market vendor and goer if they would like to trade something for his magic beans. A constable came and told him to leave the square. Prince Tyr headed north back towards the forest when he came upon a boy, leading a very unhealthy looking cow towards the market.

"Taking your milk cow to market?" Prince Tyr asked.

"Yes; I have to sell her," the boy said.

"That's too bad," Tyr said. "What's her name?"

"Abigail; mine's Jack."

"I am Tyr," the prince said.

"I'm not happy I have to sell her, but it's our last hope."

"I have hope," Tyr said. "I have it in my hand right here and I can give it to you for your milk cow."

"You can't sell hope," Jack said.

"No," Tyr said. "But you can trade it." Tyr opened his palm and showed Jack the three seeds. "These are magic beans, Jack. They will help you find all the riches you desire."

"Really?"

"Really."

Jack gave the reigns of the cow to Tyr and Tyr gave the boy the magic beans.

Tyr led the cow north; Jack went south to the market place. Back in the forest, Tyr presented the cow to Lyddia. She giggled with delight. "You will have your battle," Lyddia said. "Feige will return to his people and Edom will return to you."

"So it will be," Prince Tyr said.

Casondra Brewster

Stories are not the only thing Casondra Brewster creates. If not at her desk getting words down, she may be found in her garage banging a motorcycle into submission or concocting chef-tastic dishes in her kitchen. Besides sharing her home with the voices in her head, she resides in the Cascade Foothills with her partner, children, a shelter-rescue dog and a 55-gallon aquarium of fish that lead an enviable life of leisure.

Betrayed With a Kiss

Eric Andrews-Katz

"The sun is coming up my child," the Mother Priestess said. Her voice was soft, echoing easily off the cavern walls. Wizened grey eyes peered out from wrinkled skin and from under a faded-blue scapular and white-trimmed cowl. Three of the five other people in the cave raised their eyes to follow her finger as it pointed out daylight breaking over the desert's horizon. The remaining two neither heard nor listened, for they were dead and long ago wrapped in burial linens. "What you must do, you must decide soon. Daybreak will not wait for you to make up your mind."

"And would the answer come with the dawn, I would be that much wiser." Yoshua raised his head from where he knelt before the blue-clad crone. He looked up into the sad grey eyes that held only pity for him, quickly turning away. Standing, he brought her leathery fingers with their softer underside to his lips and kissed the back of her hands.

"What shall we do?" The youngest spoke anxiously. Te'oma ran his fingers over his face and chin, scratching his hand with his newly grown beard. "They will be searching for us before too long. We cannot continue to hide out in a burial cave."

"We all know what we cannot continue to do," growled Loudas. His dark eyes appeared menacing as they quickly captured the first few flickers of sunlight. "If you cannot offer something we can do, then do us all a favor and keep your mouth shut."

"Loudas," Yoshua said turning to face his most faithful companion. The brown ringlets of hair shimmered with each movement of his head. "We are all tired, and feel your strain. There is no reason to snap at the boy."

"Rabbi," The faithful man came forward. His sandaled feet drew small dust clouds from the heaviness of his steps. "Look again at the signs that are at hand. Fate has led us to this moment. Your followers far outnumber Rome. Not just the leaders of the 12 nomadic tribes, but now we have grown into many, and then into more. The people are looking for someone to follow and they have set their eyes on you."

"Yes, Loudas, I have heard the stories," Yoshua said. He raised his hands, cupping the cheek of his most beloved. "I have heard of this great man who enters cities with only a few loaves of bread to his name. I have heard how this angel of Heaven has transformed that humble meal into a great feast that fed the multitudes. I have heard of these great tales Loudas, but they are not about me."

"You brought them grain from foreign storage when their supply had turned to poison," Te'oma eagerly added. "That is truly feeding the masses, and in itself a miracle."

"Good Te'oma," Yoshua said. "It is kind of you to say, but your faith is betrayed by your youth."

"The people believe what they want," Loudas said. "They have long before this, and will continue to tell the stories the way they choose to remember them. If they are going to praise you for being greater than you are, why can we not use that to help our cause? Why can't we use their dedication and loyalty to rid our country of its oppressors?"

"What you suggest is rebellion," the Priestess Mari replied with perfect calm. "Rome's fist strikes hard against those that try to stand against her."

"Rome's fist strikes hard either way," Loudas snapped back. "If the people are shouting for a leader, a Messiah, why not give them what they want?"

"Because I have been to the Hill of Skulls," Yoshua calmly said. "Where once the air was filled with voices of many Messiahs, now there is a hush. The sounds that float down from there are more than the moaning wind. I do not willingly wish my own voice to join that chorus."

"Nor do I," Te'oma quickly added. His green eyes grew wide with fear and he wiped the perspiration from his brow. "Perhaps we can leave the city. Maybe we can leave the country. They will be searching for us in the Holy City. We can go around it tonight, and make our way to the East instead. Go to the lands of the Maharajas, or even further to the lands of the Mongols."

"The Eagle of Rome has sharp eyes, and a great wing span, Te'oma," Mari said from her sentinel position at the cave's mouth.

"It is not the eyes or the wings that I fear," Te'oma said.

Yoshua offered a comforting smile to the boy, a year into his manhood and less as leader of one of the 12 sacred tribes of Israel. "When the Heavenly Father walks at your side, then why should you be afraid of anything?"

Te'oma nodded and said nothing. He tried to offer a smile to show his faith, but doubt remained in his eyes, and he quickly glanced away.

"Besides, what of Phillos, and Yochanan, and all the other 8 leaders?" Yoshua asked. He spoke to the young man trying to nurture and teach instead of reprimanding. "I cannot leave Andreas, or Shimon or any of them behind to face Rome's wrath, only to seek sanctuary for myself. Tonight is the Passover Seder, and if it is to be our last time together, than let us all be together one last time. Let us celebrate the hopes of freedom from Rome, even as our ancestors fled Egypt's oppression."

"Gentle Mother," Te'oma said turning to the Priestess. "If it is true that yours is Mother of the gods, then perhaps you may whisper something into Her ear that may helps us as of yet."

The priestess offered a toothless grin and smiled at the man's innocence. "My son," she said with her every maternal instinct. "She is mother to *all* and part of the same. She watches her children get cut down with the harvest each year. How can I ask her to interfere for me?"

"Is there no one we can ask for help?" Te'oma cried.

"We can ask the great Father," Yoshua said. "That He may let the Angel of Death pass over our heads once more."

"If there is truly no one else," Te'oma said in a squeaked whisper. "Then my faith shall be my sword." He began to pray with silent fervor.

Loudas felt the frustrations building inside of him. The helpless feelings raced through his veins with a barbed edge, slicing through him with every heartbeat. Knowing there was nothing to be done, except to wait and watch as Rome tightened their fist on the their homeland.

"And what would you have us do?" Loudas' rage focused on the younger man. "Go to the Sanhedrin, the High Priests of Judea? The Pharisees who sit on their carved thrones, arguing ancient texts and

42

hiding behind their meanings? Or maybe the Seduces dressed in their silken robes and golden threads; they who spout the Holy Words while crying tears of poverty and seeking to save us from our coinage. Neither is a friend to us."

"Why not?" Te'oma defied. "We are children of Abraham and therefore they are our brothers, too. If they are not there to assist with all the children of God, then what are they there for?"

"Why indeed!" Loudas said. "The advice they would give would not be of help to anyone but them."

"If we yield to the Sacred Laws first," Te'oma argued," then we find ourselves judged by Holy Law. The Sanhedrin has no law to condemn man to death! The Scared Scriptures forbid it! What is a long jail sentence or banishment when one is looking at the sharp sword or Rome?"

"It is also forbidden in the Scriptures to heal one that is marked for the Angel of Death," Yoshua said solemnly. "But I regret not helping Lazarus to recover from the scorpion's sting."

"Saving a life is not a blasphemy," Te'oma argued. "The High Priests must recognize that?"

"They know only that I said the hidden name of God aloud, and that is an unforgivable offense." Yoshua's voice was not apologetic. "They have turned their backs on me, stripping me of my rabbinical title."

"The ancient relics can say what they want," Loudas sneered. "The people still follow you. Those pious crows are just jealous of your connection to the people. You have achieved in 30 years what they could not in 300. They argue for peace with Rome, but look to the people. The people want rebellion!"

"My most beloved," Yoshua said. His finger caressed Loudas' cheek, allowing his fingertip to trace down the center of his lips.

"Can we appeal to Herod?" The boy asked.

"The self-titled Herod the Great?" Loudas said, snarling once more at Te'oma's suggestion. "Not a drop of David's bloodline travels in his veins, but the talon of Rome gives him his crown. So he is now King of Judea. Herod will lie with Rome like a whore does with any man holding 30 pieces of silver."

"He is still a son of Abraham," Mari suggested softly from her stool of stone. "Will he listen to nothing?"

"Herod will not soon throw Rome from his eagle-feathered bed, good Mother," Loudas replied. "Do you not understand, Young Te'oma? There are three opposite powers ruling our country: Rome, the oppressor, King Herod, the bought, and High Priests, the worthless. All three are now angered. Rome has the muscle, but not the reason. Herod and the High Priests have the excuse but not the power. We have given them a single reason to unite, Yoshua ben Yusuf. Unless we can rally the 12 nomadic tribes in rebellion we are lost. Rome will not wait."

"How do you know what Rome will do?" Te'oma asked churlishly.

"I grew up in the court of Herod's father. We were in exile far away, in the very city of Rome itself. While Herod learned from Caesar's tutors, I learned how to stay out of the selection for the lions."

"How did you escape Rome's bowels?" Mari asked.

"I was befriended. By a young soldier named Marcus Serrilius." Loudas' voice broke, and he spoke just above a whisper. "He became my friend. He intervened and got me out of the selections. I moved from the pits to helping the master of arms. Marcus and I saw a lot of each other. When Herod returned to Judea with title and regiment, I was taken back with him."

"Then that's the answer from God," Te'oma proclaimed. His face took on the sunlight as it fully entered the cave. He clasped his hands together and shook them triumphantly at the cavern roof. "Praise His name high!"

"Te'oma," Yoshua asked. "What is it?"

"Marcus Serrilius," came the joyous answer. "He is Captain of the Soldiers directly under Pontius Pilatus, the 5th Prefect of Rome! Don't you see? He can assist the Rabbi in getting out of the city. He has the power to help us with a pardon. I am certain that this is the will of God."

"And you," Yoshua asked the youth softly. "You would have me sneak out of the country, like a thief in the night, and abandon those who look up to me?"

"By leaving tonight, you may still live to see tomorrow."

"The boy has a point," Loudas said. "Without you to lead, the 12 would disband and Rome would have no rebellion to crush."

"You can have time to raise a larger army," Te'oma argued with blind optimism. "When the time is right, you can come back and liberate our homeland."

"Te'oma," Yoshua said quietly. The boy waited to be praised like a faithful puppy. "I need you to be quiet."

"Rabbi?" The boy's enthusiastic joy froze on his face.

"None may know what we have discussed here." While Yoshua spoke to Te'oma, his eyes remained fixed on Loudas, observing his every movement. "You cannot tell Shimon, or any of the others, do you understand?"

"Yes, Rabbi," he answered crestfallen. "But shouldn't they know so they can cease to worry? Or make plans to join you?"

"That is why they cannot know," Yoshua said. "It is easier for a group of two or three to leave unobserved. A larger crowd would be noticed. Tonight at the Seder, I will tell them my plans to leave. What I need from you is to not doubt me. But until tonight, not a word to anyone."

"Yes Rabbi," Te'oma obediently replied.

Yoshua kissed Te'oma on the forehead. "Go and begin preparations for the Passover." The youth nodded and left the cave. No one said another word until he was out of sight.

"Rabbi," Loudas said immediately following. "You cannot expect me to appeal to that Roman dog."

"Is it true you were friends once?" Yoshua asked. The question brought an instant silence. The brown eyes studied him quietly.

The words hung in the air, supported by the thickness of the void that followed. Loudas opened his mouth to protest, and closed it with only a heavy exhaled breath.

"It is true that we were," Loudas stammered, "close once."

Yoshua cleared the distance between them. He reached out and took both of his hands in his own. "As close as we are, my beloved?"

"The boy Marcus Serrilius saved then is nothing compared to the man you know now."

"Then go to him," Yoshua asked. "Ask him to help us. I am afraid of what I have seen if I cannot turn from this path."

"Rabbi," Loudas whispered. "The Father is at your side, there is nothing to fear."

"I am afraid!" Yoshua confessed, collapsing into his arms, and clutching desperately to him. "I have heard the howling pain from the Hill of Skulls. I have heard the prayers that go unanswered as the men that say them are nailed to Roman trees. I do not want to die!" Yoshua clung tightly to Loudas, clutching so close as if to pull him inside himself, and make them one. "I know I should be brave. I should trust my Lord as my followers trust me, but I feel only fear. I have begged the Father for another path, but He has not answered, and has forsaken me." Yoshua shouted between gales of tears. "Please! If there is any other path to take: if there is any way to keep this poisoned wine from my lips, please show me! I don't want to die!"

Loudas held the shattered man against his shoulder. His body felt each sob wrack through Yoshua's flesh, shaking him into fearful convulsions. But his own body was cold with numbness, fearful of what he was seeing, and fearful of what he knew he had no other choice but to do. His love for this man was unaltered, but Loudas felt the strength of his faith fail him as it washed away like a cold rain.

"I will seek him out," Loudas said in a numbed whisper. "I will find Marcus Serrilius, and I will ask him to help."

Yoshua's sobbing quickly subsided. After a few coughs, he found his breath and regained control of his body. Taking hold of Loudas by both shoulders, Yoshua leaned back and looked his most beloved directly in the eye.

"Are you sure you can convince him to help me?" Yoshua asked without hesitation.

Loudas looked into Yoshua's brown eyes and felt a new wave of cold numbing his body. The great teacher he once idolized was nothing more than a broken man before him. "I will persuade the captain," Loudas said as he felt the air being choked from his body. He forced the answer from his mouth before the phantom constrictions about his neck prevented him from speaking. "I will promise him...anything." And he knew there would be no forgiveness.

***

The steps of the palace were made of marble. Brought in from Rome and laid before the house of the Prefect, if for no other reason, to distinguish it from any others in the area. They climbed to where two armor-plated soldiers stood sentry. A sword hung at each of their sides, along with a spear pointed skyward.

Loudas again debated whether he should make the climb or not. The street was busy with people, carts, animals and soldiers going about their business in front of the Prefect's House. Loudas saw a man coming towards him, and fearing to be recognized, pulled the hooded cloak tighter about his body and face. Realizing there was no other choice, he swallowed hard and made his way up the steps. The two guards' spears crossed his path, stopping him before he entered the building.

"What do you want, Jew?" One guard barked.

Loudas studied him first, and then his friend. He clenched his jaw, jutting his chin out, and took a deep breath before answering with control. "I need to talk to Marcus Serrilius."

"What did you say, dog?" The second guard asked. "I can't hear you when you mumble your filth. I could have sworn you asked to speak to the Captain of the Guard, his Lordship Marcus Serrilius!"

"A dog like that wouldn't know a man like the Captain of the Guard," the first soldier jibed. "If he did, he'd be sure to use the proper respectful titles for the captain."

"I didn't hear a single one of them," the second guard replied. "Shall we teach him a lesson and throw this dog down the stairs?"

Loudas pulled his lips in tightly, trying to control his anger. His hand struggled to reach for the dirk, hidden in an inner pocket sewn into the sleeve, but he managed to keep it still.

"Please," Loudas said quickly. "May I have a word with," he paused to swallow the gathering bile, and a little of his pride. "His Honor, The Captain of the Guard, Sir Marcus Serrilius of the House of Pontius Pilatus, 5th Prefect of Rome." Each word tasted of ashes.

The two soldiers looked at one another and laughed. Their game was finished. One turned around and entered the building, while the latter looked away, staring outward. An amused look lingered on his face. After what seemed a few eternal moments, the first soldier reappeared.

"Follow me, dog" came the barked order. The soldier neither encouraged nor waited for a response. He led Loudas to an open door with a linen cloth hanging in the frame. "Go," came the command, and Loudas did nothing but obey.

"Loudas Iscarri," the soldier waiting in the room identified with a deep rolling voice. "It's been many years, but I would remember that scowling look, anywhere." The soldier wore a red woolen tunic under shoulder and breastplate armor. A dagger remained attached to his belt, while his helmet lay on the tabletop behind him. His dark hair was shorn short, matching the thin beard that ran along his jawline. "Does that look of yours ever change?"

"Not very often and not for too long," came the curt answer.

Marcus Serrilius stepped aside from the table and presented a wine pitcher and a pair of goblets. "Would you like some wine?"

"No," came the answer. His body was as rigid as his words.

"Come now, Loudas," Marcus said with baited patience. "Your lack of courtesy would make your father weep."

"When it came to Rome," Loudas said, "my father wept often."

"And you," Marcus suddenly turned around until they were face to face. Loudas did not move, his expression unchanged, his eyes staring past the soldier. "Do you weep for Rome?"

Loudas stared back into the dark green eyes, fighting the anger that rose within him. When he spoke it was with emphasized clarity. "I weep for an occupied country and a conquered people." He looked past the captain, found a crack on the wall, and kept his eyes focused on the spot.

"Now that's a shame," Marcus Serrilius said. "I hoped you'd weep for me." He turned his back, letting his blood red cloak flap into Loudas' arm and hand. He poured himself some of the wine. Taking the goblet in hand, he raised it in his guest's honor and drank deeply, leaning against the table. "So if not for sentimentality sake Loudas Iscarri, what is it that brings you to see me?" His question was met with silence. After a few more moments, Marcus put the goblet on the table with an audible thud. "Your reason must be great indeed to pay for it with such hesitation." The captain helped himself to more wine. "Speak! Or do I need to have my guards help you find your tongue?"

"I need help in getting out of the country," Loudas said quickly.

"That's not a problem."

"It's not just for me," he continued. "There are others."

"How many?"

"Beside myself?"

"How many?" The captain was beginning to get irritated.

"One other," Loudas answered.

Marcus Serrilius searched the face of the man before him, and only saw the boy he knew years ago. The silent brooding of the dark haired boy that was so attractive as a youth, turned into a scowling bald man with angry eyes. It seemed to Marcus that the difference was less of a change in Loudas, and more of a metamorphosis. Either way, the man he thought so much about, over the years, was finally in front of him, and the attraction was not less. He jumped up, immediately closing the distance between the two of them.

"Who is this one other?"

"Yoshua ben Yusuf," Loudas spit out.

Marcus Serrilius stopped in place, holding his breath. His eyes closely scrutinized Loudas' face, looking for any movement, and finding none. He turned his back and found his breath, reaching for the wine goblet.

"When I first saw you, I was 12 and you were 10 years old," the captain slowly said. "You were chained at the ankle, and not more than a dingy dog. You sat apart from the others, brooding and when the chance came, you reached out and stole a coin from my father's purse. I never said a word, and he never noticed at the time. You never noticed that I saw. But I noticed you."

Loudas lowered his eyes, along with his shoulders, for the first time since entering. "I remember a boy with eyes as green as the tree tops, and hair as golden as sunlight. He followed his father into the dungeons looking for a house slave."

"I was the one that convinced him to take you." Marcus scoffed. "If he only knew what he was giving me."

"I have no fond memories of your father," Loudas abruptly interrupted.

"So few do," Marcus agreed.

"I see you wear the ring of your Father's House."

"He gave it to me on my 17th name day."

"As a sign of your devotion?"

"To show his support at my wedding." Marcus returned to the flagon of wine.

Loudas spoke after much hesitation. "I'm sure your father is very proud."

"I can only imagine," Marcus answered. "He's dead."

"And your loving wife?"

"She's not dead," Marcus said with another sip of wine. "She is in Rome."

"And you?"

"I have chosen affairs of the army over affairs of the heart. I am Captain of the Soldiers, and I am in Judea. Now, I am glad of all three factors." He drained the goblet for a final time. "But you do not need me to tell you of my titles, or else you would not be here asking such a favor."

"I did not know you were married or that your father is dead."

"Does that matter?" Marcus asked.

After a sharp pause Loudas answered. "No."

"But you are here asking me to smuggle an outlaw out of the country?"

"Rabbi Yoshua ben Yosef is not an outlaw!"

"I am very familiar with his exploits," Marcus snapped back. He counted off offenses on his fingers. "Speaking out against Caesar. He's been plotting with the leaders of the 12 tribes to rebel against Rome, and that is forbidden. He is a rabble-rouser guilty of sedition. And that is just the complaints from Rome. You should hear what Herod or the Sanhedrin say."

"Yoshua is not an outlaw."

"No? Then what is he?" Marcus asked. "The Messiah? Go up to Golgotha and walk among the broken men who claimed they were Messiahs as well. There are many there and yet, not one has proven true."

"So there is nothing you will do." It was not a question. Loudas turned and started for the doorway.

"You will wait until you are dismissed before leaving my office!" Marcus Serrilius commanded. He slowly made his way to where Loudas remained standing. Putting a hand on his shoulder, Marcus slid between his guest and the door. "I have authority. I can help your friend."

Loudas remained perfectly still. His eyes cut a look towards the captain studying his face. "You *can* help or you *will* help?" His tone was sharp, but he kept his control.

"Both." Marcus put his free hand on Loudas' other shoulder. The smile that crossed his lips was not to be trusted. "I have something in mind."

Loudas stepped back and allowed his self to be guided back into the room.

"The favor you ask is not a small task," Marcus began. "Your Yoshua has angered a lot of people."

"When a people are oppressed, what other feeling can there be but anger?"

"I suggest you learn to control yours before we continue." Marcus reached up and let the back of his finger brush down Loudas face. "That's better. Now, what I propose is this. You tell me where, and I'll meet the both of you, with a few of my guards. We'll get you out of the country."

"You need to come alone," Loudas said.

"And what is to prevent the lot of you from holding me hostage or killing me when I appear?"

Loudas thought a moment. "We haven't discussed our plan with any of the others. The wine will be lightly sedated and there will be no fight. By the time they come to full senses, we will be long gone."

"You would abandon them so easily?" Marcus asked curiously.

"Our cause is lost," Loudas said. "If nothing else, meeting with you has proven that. When Yoshua is gone, the rest will return to their lives as fisherman and shepherds."

"Will you give me your word of honor that it will be the last time we hear of your rebellion?"

"Remove the head and the body will fall," Loudas said. "Once away, Yoshua's interest will change. We are not meant to liberate our country. Others will have to do it in our stead."

Marcus nodded solemnly. "I will meet you alone. I'll have tunics, sandals, cloaks, food and wine for you both, enough to get you to the borders of Judea and off to Damascus. The rest is up to you."

"And what do you want in return?" Loudas asked quickly.

Marcus' smile was slowly drawn out. "Bringing an end to this rebellion will bring me glory and honor in my Prefect's eyes."

"You do all this for glory?"

"All is done for glory," Marcus Serrilius answered.

"Tonight," Loudas said quietly. "After the Passover Seder. He will be alone, praying in the private garden of Gethsemane Inn. Once you identify yourself to him, we will follow you."

"How will I know which one is he?"

He thought a moment. "I shall give him a kiss, and you will know."

***

Loudas left the dinner celebration to follow the path to the gardens. The sounds of the others faded as he closed the private gate, entering the clearing. In the center of the garden, he found Yoshua rising from prayer. Slowly, he approached placing his hand gently on the small of the Rabbi's back.

"Are they asleep yet?" Yoshua asked.

"They are well on their way," Loudas answered. "Mari's wine should make them sleep until we are far away."

"And where has she gone?"

"The Priestess has taken Te'oma away," Loudas said. "He can deny being any part of this without being called craven."

"So there is nothing now but to wait," Yoshua said, eyes looking upward and scanning the star-filled skies. He kept his back to him. "It will be good to see the land of the Maharajas again. Their Rabbis have so much to teach us. Will you study the sacred texts also, or will you look for work elsewhere?"

There was a long silence before Loudas answered. "I will not be going with you." A second silence joined them. "I will see you to Damascus, but then I must return here."

"Return to your rebellion?" Yoshua asked without facing him.

"It is what I have pledged myself to do," Loudas answered. "It is the path I must follow."

Yoshua turned to look his companion in the eyes. He saw the struggle Loudas internally fought, and immediately knew that his most faithful companion was lost to him.

"Being who you are," Yoshua said softly. "You can do nothing else." He placed his hands on Loudas' shoulders.

Loudas ignored the sounds of feet approaching from behind him. He moved his hands to Yoshua's shoulders and the two men stood connected, hands to shoulders, staring in each other's eyes. Loudas leaned forward and kissed Yoshua's lips.

"You are my most beloved," one said to the other, and it was understood between them.

"Yoshua ben Yusuf," came the voice of Marcus Serrilius. "You are under arrest for leading rebellions against Rome."

Yoshua looked into Loudas' eyes with confusion. "You would betray me?"

"No, Rabbi," Loudas frantically whispered. "Not I!"

Five soldiers surrounded them in a circle, spears pointed inwards and swords in hand. Two took hold of Yoshua by his arms.

"You have betrayed me." It wasn't a question; it was declaration.

"No," Loudas protested as the soldiers lead Yoshua out of the garden. He looked back meeting his eyes only for an instant, before turning and being taken away.

Loudas reached for his dirk and started towards Marcus Serrilius. Two soldiers stepped between them, swords in hand.

"I wouldn't come closer, Loudas," Marcus said between his two guards. "These men are looking for an excuse to kill your pack of dogs. The same goes for all of you!" The captain raised his voice and looked about the edges of the garden. Three of the apostles had awoken and were helplessly watching. The strong wine allowed only a limp grasp on their swords. The dirk fell from Loudas' hand. The soldiers raised their weapons, showing they were ready to fight.

"Why?" Loudas asked. It was all he could say.

Marcus stepped between his guards until he was eye to eye with him. Without warning, he took hold of Loudas by the sides of his head and pulled him close. Their lips met hard, teeth cutting flesh bringing a subtle taste of blood. Loudas did not struggle and Marcus held his head firmly in place.

"Why would you do this?" Loudas quietly beseeched.

"As you told me, 'Remove the head and the body will fall'," Marcus answered. "There is no more reason for concern."

"You have left me nothing," Loudas mumbled in quiet shock.

"I did it for you," was the reply.

"You have betrayed me," Loudas said.

"I am here for you," Marcus fiercely replied.

"I cannot," Loudas said. "I cannot go with him. I cannot stay here."

"Come with me," Marcus said. "We can be together."

"No!" Loudas said. "We cannot. I am not a whore. You have left me nothing!"

Marcus Serrilius studied Loudas for several long moments. "You're a fool," was all he said.

The captain of the guard snapped around and started off. Before exiting the garden he turned around to face Loudas. Reaching into his cloak, he withdrew a coin purse. Weighing it in his hand, the captain tossed it lightly over to where Loudas stood watching. Silver coins spilled out across the garden grounds like pieces of a shattered moon.

"Fool or whore," Marcus Serrilius said. "You have earned your wage." He proceeded to follow his guards and left the garden.

Loudas looked around at the faces of the remaining apostles. He saw the effects of the wine, the fear in their eyes and the anger on their faces.

"They will never understand the truth," Loudas whispered with fear. "They will blame me. They will call me damned."

Loudas Iscarri ran into the night. He knew the others would not follow. Come morning, they would be hunted by Rome. Loudas felt the wind biting his face as he ran. It stung his skin and brought tears to his eyes. Everything he wanted, everything he had fought for was lost. He was left with nothing, except an oppressed country and a shattered faith.

Eric Andrews-Katz

lives in Seattle with his partner Alan. His first story, *"Mr. Grimm's Faery Tale"* was a 2008 Spectrum Short Fiction Award nominee, published in *So Fey: Queer Fairy Fiction* (2008 Lambda Literary nominee). Other works appear in: *The Best Date Ever, Charmed Lives: Gay Spirit in Storytelling, Gay City: Vols 2 & 3,* and *Zombiality: A Queer Bent on the Undead* (all Lambda Literary nominees). Eric's first novel *The Jesus Injection* is to be released by Bold Strokes Press in 2012. You can find Eric at: *www.EricAndrewsKatz.com*

How Should I Presume

Charles Green

And indeed there will be time/To wonder "Do I dare?" and, "Do I dare?"

The question rang in my ears as I saw Peter, lunch in hand, approaching the tables, raising his slender arm to brush a stray strand of long, blonde hair into place.

I looked up from The Love Song of J. Alfred Prufrock, my palms sweaty with anticipation. Here was another chance to talk to this incredible seventh grader who had caught my attention only a week earlier. I burned to walk the two feet separating us, and talk with Peter about where he wanted to go to college, his favorite books, current events. Anything I could think of. And I wanted to hear what he had to say, wanted to listen to that sweet voice that took my breath away every time I heard it. But I remembered the terrible impression I made the night before, and knew Peter would never want to talk to me again.

I took a deep breath. I had to read Prufrock before class, so I turned back to the poem. I tried to pick up where I left off, but kept glancing around to watch the golden-haired boy eating and talking, completely oblivious to my predicament. I thought back to the first time I laid eyes on this remarkable boy. It was so recent and yet, I felt as though I knew him all my life.

I had been basking in the Los Angeles sun, trying to tan my pale face and arms, and gazing out at the athletic field. A few minutes passed before I heard the masses of hungry teenagers scurrying from classes, eager for lunch. I watched as they found places on the picnic benches to sit, my arms folded across my chest, not looking at anything in particular.

Suddenly, a young boy, his bronze skin perfect for capturing the sun's rays, strolled into my sight, toward one of the benches. Jolting me out of my contemplation, I leaned forward expectantly. I stared with my mouth open at the boy's light blonde hair, hung in long bangs to frame his eyes, a shade of blue I only noticed before in paintings of the Pacific.

As he sat down, pulling out his maroon polo shirt from his khaki pants, what really drew me to stare was his smooth, almost feminine face. It was as though he were a Greek statue come to life, a male Pygmalion given flesh and bone by some divine power. He didn't notice my intense adoration, as we were sitting some distance, and he was soon involved in an intense conversation with a friend, gesturing with one hand while holding his food with the other.

After an eternity I realized I was gawking at this young man like a country boy having seen skyscrapers for the first time, and whipped my head back toward the field in embarrassment. I passed my hands through my thick, brown hair, struggling with the strange new feelings aroused by this boy. At once the desire came over to march right up and introduce myself. But I looked at my wrinkled, unwashed T-shirt, stooped posture, and flecks of hair hanging from my chin, and knew the boy would keep silent, or even shout for a teacher, if I approached him.

Even more, I realized I knew nothing about this young man, not even his name. After thinking about the situation, wanting to speak to this Adonis but needing to know more about him, I decided to see what I could learn. Having made up my mind, I turned around and gazed at the boy all through lunch, imprinting on my mind his sun-drenched skin, his loud belly-laugh, his habit of massaging his neck with long, slender fingers.

The bell jolted me back to reality, and I realized I had spent my entire lunch staring at this boy. If I didn't hurry, I would miss class. With great regret I raced for my classroom, brushing close enough to the boy's bench to overhear the friend he had been talking to, about to rush off himself, utter, "Bye, Peter."

I pumped the air with my fist. I knew his first name! Now all I needed was a last name, and I could approach him. I knew where I could get that information, but in the meantime I would have to sit through several classes. It would be worth the wait.

When I got home, I raced to my room, anxious to pour over the yearbook. My hand was on the closet door when I halted, my heart pounding in surprise to find my mother turning down the sheets of my bed.

"Hi, sweetheart," she said, tucking in the corners. "How was school?"

"Fine," I replied, trying to sound natural. I debated whether to tell her about the day's events. I always had a good relationship with my parents. I could usually discuss anything with them. But the prospect of talking to them about Peter and these unfamiliar feelings made me feel as though I were confessing to a murder. I could feel the blood rushing to my face as I struggled to decide what to tell her. At the same time I silently prayed she would leave so I could check the yearbook.

Finally, I made my choice. Having finished the sheets, my mother walked over to me and wrapped her arms around my chest. It was a family ritual. We hugged each other at every opportunity, and normally I relished it. But today I wanted to be alone with my mental picture of this young man, and so my return of the gesture was perfunctory, my large hands lightly touching her back.

"Anything exciting happen today?" she asked. It was the question I dreaded, and had to answer. I took a deep breath, screwed up my courage, and lied.

"No, same old stuff," I said, feeling guilty the moment the words left my mouth. I thought for sure she would realize I wasn't telling her everything, but she didn't notice. She just gave my shoulder a little squeeze and walked out, her business there finished.

As soon as she left, I raced into the closet and grabbed the yearbook. I flipped it open to the middle school section and began carefully examining the pictures from each grade. As I glanced through the photos, doubt about my motives crept into my mind. I began to wonder why I hadn't just introduced myself to Peter when I first saw him. I was equally concerned with my hesitation in telling my mother about him. I hated lying, especially to my parents, and the fact that I felt I had to do that made me consider whether I should really be pursuing this boy. Was Peter worth all this effort, if I had to sneak around my own family?

I temporarily silenced my thoughts when I came across Peter in the sixth grade section. There was no chance mistaking those huge, blue eyes, which held me in a trance. Comparing the photo with my mental image, I knew with absolute certainty they were of the same person. I looked at the caption below.

"Donaldson, Peter," it read. "Peter Donaldson," I whispered, repeating the name like a mantra.

I then flipped through the rest of the yearbook, searching for any extracurricular activities Peter might belong to. I soon found him in the orchestra's group photo. I gazed at this young man's perfect face, sighing deeply at the thought of speaking with him, of maybe even hearing him play the violin tucked in his arms.

The next few days, whenever I had the chance, I sat outside on the benches, doing my homework while waiting for Peter to walk by between classes, sit down for lunch, or play soccer on the field. I saw several chances to speak to him, but hesitated each time, too fearful of Peter's possible reaction. I didn't want anyone in school branding me gay, and I hadn't observed Peter long enough to know whether he would jump to that conclusion. I needed to be sure before taking such a risk. So I kept back, waiting for the perfect opportunity.

I also began to spend more time on my appearance, combing my hair, shaving the few whiskers on my chin, taking little bites of food and chewing slowly. I wanted to make a good impression when I finally spoke to Peter. My mother noticed the difference and asked if I had a girlfriend. "No," I replied definitively, ending the discussion. I never told my parents about Peter. I could never explain why, but I wanted to keep this incredible young man to myself.

Finally, I noticed on a bulletin board that the orchestra would be performing that Thursday. When I read the notice, I wanted to burst into song. I knew this was the chance I had been waiting for. That night, I convinced my parents to let me borrow the car for the performance. I told them some of my friends were playing. Indeed, a few people I knew were involved. But my attention would be solely focused on Peter.

Thursday night finally came, and I sat, tapping my foot in anticipation in the crowded auditorium. I craned my neck around the stage, hoping to catch a glimpse of Peter and confirm he was there. Unfortunately, I could barely see the stage over the rows of talking heads. The concert eventually started, and I straightened up even more, almost rising out of my seat as the musicians marched on-stage. I spotted Peter, his full, red lips open in a wide grin. I settled back in my seat, quietly releasing the breath I hadn't realized I was holding.

As the orchestra began to play, I leaned back in my chair, closing my eyes and savoring the soft, breathtaking melody. All the anxiety from thinking about Peter drained from my body. I let my arms and neck go limp. I lost myself in the music, almost forgetting my purpose in attending.

At the end of the concert, though, I quickly got up from my seat, and hurried to the lunch area, where several benches were arranged with sodas. I pushed and shoved my way to the front, so I would have an excellent view. I waited to intercept Peter before anyone else, too apprehensive to get a drink even though my throat was parched. I wondered if he was going to show, or if he had left already. My heart sunk as the minutes ticked by with no sign of the boy, and I was ready to leave when suddenly a familiar voice from behind asked, "Excuse me?"

I turned around to face the bronzed boy himself, standing with his head nearly even with my heart, dressed in a black blazer and slacks with a blue dress shirt and red bow tie. He was so near I could glimpse faint traces of what my grandmother playfully called "peach-fuzz" on his upper lip.

I had to stifle my delight, clamping my jaw shut and forcing myself to remain calm. I prayed for this opportunity all week, but now, to be so close to Peter, to be able to talk to him, I couldn't think of anything to say. My mouth felt wired shut, and my legs were rooted to the ground. I had to respond, so I took a deep breath and, summoning all my willpower, forced myself to say, "Yes?"

"Could I get a soda, please?" the golden-haired boy asked, brushing a stray strand of hair out of his eyes. He was so close the warmth of his breath tingled on my hands.

"S-sure," I replied. I grabbed a bottle from the bench and handed it to Peter. "Thank you," he said, his eyes staring into me, drawing me in and forcing me to turn away for an instant before I could continue.

"No problem," I nodded, the only motion I could perform. Peter unscrewed the lid and took a sip, sighing in pleasure when he was finished. I knew I had to say something else if I wanted to keep his interest. My voice trembling, I said, "Congratulations, you played well."

"Thanks," he said again, taking another sip of soda and smiling, pleased with the compliment. My mind raced for something else to say, but I was so overwhelmed with the intensity of the moment, of this golden-haired young man actually speaking to me, that my mind went blank. I wiped away invisible perspiration from my forehead, hoping to inspire more words, but nothing happened. The two of us stood staring at each other like victims of Medusa, turned to stone.

After what seemed like forever, a shrill voice called out nearby, "Peter! Come over here, please!" jolting us out of our collective trance.

"I gotta go," Peter said, frowning in disappointment. "Thanks for the drink."

"Bye," I whispered as he turned and walked away, raising my hand in a half-hearted gesture. Peter strolled over toward a tall woman in a blue dress. I assumed she was his mother. I realized I wouldn't get another chance to talk to him again that night, so I left. I was delighted at having actually spoken with Peter, but also angry for standing there silently like a fool, not even telling him my name.

On the way home I cursed my nervousness, thinking of all the questions I could have asked about his musical talents. I wanted to kick myself for blowing a perfect opportunity. I figured he would never want to talk to me again after that evening, and my eyes welled up when I realized my only recourse for the next year and a half was observing Peter from a distance, and fantasizing about what might have happened.

I snapped back to the present moment, staring at the golden-haired boy munching on a sandwich, not ten steps away, his green polo shirt hanging loose over his shorts. I turned back to Prufrock, trying to focus on the poem and not making much progress. I so desperately wanted to get up and walk over to Peter's bench, to talk with this young man and rekindle the spark I knew was there. But I was scared. I couldn't stand the thought of Peter rejecting me, and how else would he react to someone who clammed up during their first conversation? I gripped the book tighter in frustration.

I was determined to finish the poem, and turned back to its pages. Trembling, I read "Do I dare/Disturb the universe?/In a minute there is time/For decisions and revisions which a minute will reverse." I took a deep breath, amazed at the relevance. I stole another glance at Peter, wondering again about my chances and what I felt for the boy. Still unsure, I returned to Prufrock, sharply inhaling as I saw lines which spoke directly to me, every word infused with an intense sense of regret, frustration, and loss.

Quickly finishing the poem, I slammed the book shut and jumped to my feet, bursting with newfound energy. I would not end up like Prufrock, alone and mourning missed opportunities. Now or never, I thought. I marched over to Peter. Whatever happened, I would not look back with regret. If I was meant to connect with him, it would happen now. If not, I would finally know and could move on. I seemed to grow taller as Peter gazed up at me, recognition passing over his face. Putting down his soda, the bronzed boy smiled, and tossed his head back, waiting for me to speak. I returned the gesture, and opened my mouth, after quickly putting my thoughts in order.

"Hi," I said, swallowing down my remaining fear, "remember me?"

Charles Green

is a writer and editor based in Annapolis, Maryland. His articles and reviews have appeared in many publications, including *The Gay & Lesbian Review*, Lambda Literary Foundation website, and *Publishers Weekly*. Two of his magazine articles won Honorable Mention in the 78th annual *Writers Digest* Writing Competition.

The Not So Odd Couple

Byron Darden

A cool breeze deflects the sun's hot rays upon two lovers sitting on the beach. They peacefully rest beside one another as they peer out over the steel blue hue of the Puget Sound. In the distance, the faint sound of a conductors whistle blows in the air as a train approaches prompting both men to respond. One is significantly older, somewhat stout and dressed stylishly European even when sunbathing.

The other man is an athletically fit and younger mixed race bookworm thumbing through a new manuscript beautifully bound in contrasting colors of sun burnt orange and royal blue. Neither gentlemen is a slob yet both could not be more different from the other in true Odd Couple fashion, except for the striking resemblance they share as though related to one another in the way that people spending time together can sometimes project to onlookers.

One says to the other, "Why in the hell would they build a railroad along the coast line? There's already so much waterfront property that the general public can't get to." He takes a sip of his frosted beer in contrast to the heat that surrounds him. It is hot out, yet the cool breeze whisks across their skin raising goose bumps as the heat of the sun's rays beats down on the drying sand surrounding them.

"Now they go and build a train that runs along the shoreline restricting easy access and ruining the picturesque view of the western sky just beyond the mountain range. It doesn't make sense." He continues once again, as he's prone to finding the shadow side of any particular situation.

At first glance nothing could be more obvious than the thoughtless building of the railroad in this location. The couple already accesses the beach by illegally crossing the railroad tracks now occupied by the passing train. The one lover is annoyed at the complication on his life to which the railroad path contributes. It seems more reasonable to build the tracks through the city. That way the two fellows would have greater access to the water's edge than is currently available. It is so obvious to the questioning partner, Oscar that rethinking the railroad location makes more sense.

The other lover, Felix, turns to Oscar and empathizes with his sentiment that the railroad hugs the coastline leaving most residents hungry for greater access to its shores. There are also more considerations to ponder; something Oscar tends to overlook.

"Like what?" replies Oscar, his eyebrows furrowing inward toward each other like apposing skis about to no longer support their master, edging toward an inevitable spill?

Taking a drink of his beer as though scrutinizing the qualities of a fine wine from a crystal goblet as he furrows one brow in apparent ecstasy, Felix swirls the cool liquid in his mouth before swallowing and responds, "There's something romantic about the picture you've painted of the train's path." Felix whispers the words as if they are creating delicate brush stokes on a fresh canvas.

"I can see the seamless transition of the lush green landscape unfolding before my eyes as I gaze out the window from my seat. The way the light dances on the Puget Sound as the waves ebb and flow like ballerinas floating across the stage. It seems magical in my mind as I notice how the Olympic peaks jet up piercing the low cloud cover," Felix continues gesturing broadly with his outstretched arms with a reflective twinkle in his eye mirroring the movement of the water.

"Like priceless Italian frescos displayed in the grand hall of the Louvre Museum. Simply breath taking," Felix, sighs as if revitalized from heightened sexual lovemaking, his mind wondering back to the Parisian home of priceless beauty. For a moment Oscar is speechless.

"You've got an overactive imagination," quips Oscar pragmatically as he takes another hardy butch gulp of his Corona followed by a loud belch.

"I said it's a pretty train ride. I never meant to make it sound like wild sex," continues Oscar.

"You see," gasps Felix responding in unison with the piercing shriek of the passing train's whistle just beyond the grove of gnarly pines separating the tracks from the secluded stretch of beach frequented by scantily clad homosexuals on which the two men lay lounging.

"Even you experienced the sexual gratification of the passenger train ride, but without the wild part," says Felix who then takes a breath before continuing. "Instead I experience it as a sensual, loving rejuvenation like the cigarette that follows… if I smoked of course. Yuck!" With each descriptive word Felix' voice deepens and becomes breathier right up to the point of the disdain he demonstrates at the thought of nicotine sucking back into his lungs. "And that's just my own selfish appreciation for those tracks remaining right where they are," exhales Felix in contentment as he burrows into the sand with his ass creating a comfortable cradle in which to support his lower back.

Oscar lifts his body up off his beach towel to rest on his ashy elbows; his sun drenched salt and pepper chest hairs glistening from perspiration. He looks over at Felix, head cocked to one side away from Felix, his expression seems to say, 'Are you kidding me? Its just a train ride for Christ's sake, point 'a' to 'b.' Drama Queen!' Oscar drops back onto his towel, shaking his head as though talking to someone obviously out of touch with reality.

"I'm telling you Felix," says Oscar as his head presses into the earth in a useless attempt at convincing his head turning boyfriend. "It's a waste of real estate having that fucking train keep us from getting to what little beach there is to enjoy. Then again coming from the likes of you, I guess I can't expect you to have the same perspective." Oscar purses his lips in disapproval.

"And exactly what is that suppose to mean, 'coming from the likes of me?' What are you trying to say, Oscar?" Felix' voice begins to sound irritated. "That I'm not entitled to my opinion? Or…"

"There you go again with all your endless questions," snaps back Oscar as he tires of this routine of one-upmanship that drives a wedge of separateness between them.

"You can't fix everything nor make sense of all the ways of the world." Oscar takes a breath and then continues. "I just want to say what's on my mind. I don't need a lecture. A little peace and quite, a couple of beers, maybe a little slap and tickle," Oscar's code word for sex.

"Then on to the next thing is all I want. Can't it just be that simple?" Oscar quiets hoping the subject is finished.

The images that Felix conjures up with his mind almost appear projected in his eyes as he describes his excitement at the thought of sex, "The Fucking Train! Now that's an idea. Gets my motor running. It's an orgy on the Oral Express against the backdrop of the coastline as passengers romp their way to Canada."

Oscar takes a deliberate breath, collecting his thoughts before speaking to the benefits of rerouting the train in an attempt to shift back to the subject at hand. "Besides, if the train went through town, it would be more accessible to passengers, easier for cargo pick up & delivery and you save time and money by cutting out the winding path Mr. Locomotion has to travel by being way the hell out here. Makes sense."

Felix furrows the other brow pondering the practical aspect of Oscar's view, then sheepishly sighs, "I see your point. Just the same, you still have that whistle noising up the atmosphere. And there's the addition of heavier traffic making its way amongst railroad crossings," Felix continues gesturing articulately with his image creating hands gently dancing in the air like an orchestral conductor directing a sonant, "delays and numerous riders trying to get a 'free ride.' That 'not paying for the ride' routine impacts those of us who don't frequent the train ride, you know." Nearly out of breath, Felix manages to eek out one last point, "We pay the price of those free loaders."

"What do you care Felix. You've never even ridden the train!" Oscar spits out his reply in full roll-of-the-eyes disbelief.

How often could an unlikely pair find themselves embroiled in senseless argument before recognizing how their differences plague their existence as a couple? It's an age-old question and an indication of how we can sometimes contemplate attempting to fit a square peg in a round hole, possibly entertaining at best if you have the right lubrication to grease the path for a tenable relationship.

"All I'm saying is, there are as many good reasons for the train to be exactly where it is, on the coastline where less impact is felt by the folks in a community – very possibly troubled by a train rolling through their neighborhood." Felix takes a deep breath on the brink of giving up reasoning with a beer slugging Oscar.

What is it about a long-term relationship that goes south once one or the other of the couple discover one day that they awaken next to a stranger? What triggers the honeymoon veil to be whisked away by a strong wind revealing the naked truth about the other person you thought you knew at the time you committed to the relationship? How can two people, seemingly so very much in synch, suddenly find themselves on the sandy soil of the beach overtaken by floodwaters when the tide rolls in?

Curious fact about seeing things as if for the first time, it turns out to be the second and often far more times than we might think, just with wiser eyes, evolved feelings and needs more clarified in our minds. We sometimes only focus on a limited set of wants and desires that we believe to hold the greatest importance. Then life unfolds and before we know it, a much longer list of wants and desires unmet for far too long, come spilling out like loose change falling out of a hole, well warn into the seam of the pant's pocket. There at the foot of the spewing fountain of coins sits a beggar we just told moments ago, we had nothing to share. Oops, there it is!

Then there is the veil we carry around covering ourselves like a shield from the outside world. We wear it like sunglasses on a less than sunny day allowing us to cruise the guy that walks by on the street. We stroll along thinking 'Mr. Guy' is non the wiser. We forget that our mouths are now dropped open to our chest in awe of the package this hunk is sporting proudly in his jeans, that he has just now flexed for our cruising eyes. Oops, caught you looking! We just never expect the wind to be strong enough to blow our cover anymore than Marilyn Monroe sheepishly intended her dress to take wind in *The Seven-Year Itch.*

Thank God for the solid ground upon which we THINK we stand promising us a successful union with Mr. Wonderful passing by, only to discover he isn't *all that nor a bag of chips.* What we really end up with is the sea salt that should have been in the bag. Instead that salt lies mixing with the sand surrounding us on the beach where we lay sunning ourselves…until the high tide.

Then we learn the way back from the beach is blocked by floodwaters spewing in from the Puget Sound thus soaking our towels and spirit when all we were trying to do is offer a different perspective on where the train tracks should be laid. Who knew we could see things so differently! In fact, everything we see is entirely based on our own experiences. We can only see the other's view if we step far enough back to recognize there indeed is a forest made up of all those trees. Behind the trees is a surprise, the impact of which may only result in a train ride along the waterfront or through town.

"What do you think of grabbing a bite to eat in town on the way home, Felix?" Oscar suggests matter-of-fact.

Somewhat smug Felix shoots back, "You mean among the loud train engine horns and the traffic delays?" Felix raises an eyebrow; beginning to seethe at the thought of throwing off the delicate balance he over exaggerates Oscar to possess. "How could I dream of partaking in such sacrilege as to upset your Chi, or whatever you call it."

"Chi? Are you still mad about my wanting a Chi tea latte when you wanted me to abstain from drinking milk?" Oscar quips realizing old wounds that have obviously never fully healed. "Face it Felix, mad cow disease is the least of our worries. Let it go for goodness sake. We've been around that topic so often I'm beginning to churn into butter."

Felix takes a deep breath in acceptance that continuing to beat on that drum only creates more noise in an already tumultuous relationship. "Oh, OK. I'll let it go if you can just tell me one thing? Did or did you not cease to have irritable bowel syndrome once you stopped drinking the milk? Admit it! Felix drops the pitch of his voice along with the lowering of his chin, staring directly in Oscar's direction waiting for his point to be proven.

"Felix, what point are you trying to make?" says Oscar as if he has no idea what the answer to the question is now posed to him.

Felix lifts his chin, stretches his neck upwards and purses his lips in anticipation of Oscars reply to his own question. A caught red handed Oscar resigns he will not get any rest until he admits what both lovers already know.

"Alright Felix, yes, the irritable bowel stopped when the dairy ceased. You happy?" Oscar once again falls under the spell of the often smug, 'see, I was right again' self-righteous air surrounding Felix like an undisputed aura of superiority. Another verbal boxing match comes to an end as Felix drinks in satisfaction if only for a moment.

"Now its just YOU that causes my bowels to be irritable," Oscar half whispers pretending Felix is unable to hear the comment spoken with ample volume to the contrary.

Felix begins expressing his indignation as it surfaces to the top like heat rising on a hot summer day of a hot desert pavement. This is right where Oscar purposely tries to lure him. Only Felix is able to outwit

Oscar by pulling back in defense so as not to fall into Oscars needling temptation to start a fight. And so the banter stalls.

Then with the precision of a linguistic surgeon Felix questions, "Oscar, your stomach rumbling?"

Exhausted from the back in forth needling at each other's nerves, the couple takes a long look at one another seemingly satisfied with their mutual attack. A passer by might assume an argument of significant importance had reached its peak only to find the odd couple loosing steam and interest in continuing to argue; then realizing…a fencing match of sorts has just been completed.

The couple rises from their towels, gather their belongings and take a long sigh as they pack their bags. It's time to depart the beach. The older of the two brushes the sand off what appears to be a briefcase historically seen carried by an old time lawyer. The leather is worn. The handles are dull from the oils of the skin rubbing a burnished finish from years of use. The younger man slips the manuscript back into his knapsack, his hand grazing the royal blue cover with his finger as it brushes against the orange accent. He slips on his sandals and turns to the other and says, "Dad, not only do I think you're cool for accepting me as your gay son, I've thoroughly enjoyed learning the finer points of being a better actor from you."

The young man's father smiles with a chuckle, "Well, thank you son. Arguing a case well in the courtroom was a hard learned lesson I got in acting class. As for accepting you, if it weren't for your mother's preparing me years ago for your news of coming out, I'd a missed out on growing old getting to know you. Now let's get the hell out of this heat and get something to eat!"

The not so odd couple crossed the tracks with the delicacy of building multiple layers of a wedding cake, carful not to loose balance upon the loose rock and aging railroad ties. Oscar's stout frame ambled along the narrow path that lay beside the tracks taking care not to stumble along the way. Felix leading the charge being sure to guide his dad away from the steep grade as they moved from the lower track to the higher one at its side. They headed up the hill from the tracks and turned to take one last look at the cool waters of the Puget Sound. Summer had come to an end. The fall winds began to blow in as the duo headed home.

Byron Darden

is a leadership development consultant coaching fortune 500 corporate executives on communications skills and leadership behaviors by raising awareness on diversity and implementing performance techniques honed in the professional performing arts and sports industries. Darden is a double master rated figure skating coach, professional actor and has worked for nearly a decade in the corporate sector globally. He is currently writing his first book of stories illustrating the path to succeeding at your goals.

Benvolio:

A Play in Development

Craig Martin

Back-story to Shakespeare's Romeo and Juliet—Benvolio, Romeo's kinsman and best friend, has a closely kept secret. Their friend, the ever-curious Mercutio, seeks to learn what it is.

Night. A Verona street.

(Benvolio and Mercutio remain in the wake of revelers.)

BENVOLIO: Romeo, Romeo, disappeared. Gone from the merriment of Capulet's feast. Gone into the night. Gone to what venture I'll not try to guess.

MERCUTIO: Sweet Benvolio, I'll venture to guess a lady has caught his eye, his story this night as old as time.

BENVOLIO: Let Romeo have his night and secret passion. You and I, Mercutio, will have the telling of it on the morrow.

MERCUTIO: Wait! What of Benvolio's 'secret passion'? Speak not of Romeo's secrets while you have a secret of your own. You tease the truth. Tell what young maiden has your secret eye.

BENVOLIO: Aye, there's a secret. Yet what secret be a secret once it's told? Pray, Mercutio, query me not.

MERCUTIO: As we be friends, tell what secret scandal holds your heart?

BENVOLIO: My heart true is held, but my wit is held from telling, for there would be the heart of scandal.

MERCUTIO: Scandal is oft companion to love, yet all love to hear scandal. Tell me! Tell me! In trade I'll swear none other shall hear.

BENVOLIO: I tell you this: it's someone fills my life, all but this tiny place of willing telling. My heart's desire knows no more than my simple affection. In friendship, Mercutio, ask no more.

MERCUTIO: How shall this passion find room in your heart without telling?

BENVOLIO: True, 'tis a secret yearns to be out, shadowing me like an invisible companion, craving acknowledgement. But how?

MERCUTIO: Here's the way: Let imagination certify your passion. Imagine me not Mercutio, but your beloved. In that guise I'll listen. Though your affections be not widely heard, my private listening may give them voice.

BENVOLIO: How do I see you without seeing my Mercutio? And yet if I am sometimes blinded by passion, I think my eyes accept this ruse.

(Mercutio turns 360 degrees, now facing him as Benvolio's beloved.)

MERCUTIO: Come, then. I am flattered by your attention, and would know the precision of it.

BENVOLIO: Mercutio, good friend, I'll trick my eyes and seeing you, imagine you my secret love.

MERCUTIO: Mercutio? That scoundrel has gone and left me in his place. Let me know all the thoughts your secret mind has thought of me. Keep close those thoughts no longer. Let us be close in truth.

BENVOLIO: In truth I would say, "My Heaven! My Star! My brilliant comet that blossoms in the night. Your one steady self directs my path."

MERCUTIO: I am truly moved to know how fond you are of me.

BENVOLIO: Say not merely fond, but foundered. Nor tide, nor ocean's wave may move me from this desire.

MERCUTIO: Tell what about me so captures your heart.

BENVOLIO: I cannot tell thee. Our language lacks the words. Yet I tell thee: Each fine curl of hair that floats above your wise brow, sweet rosebud lips I pray will blossom, teasing, against my cheek. Yet most of all I love your sweet and gentle disposition.

MERCUTIO: In trade I tell you what these eyes adore: Benvolio's grace and happy strength of purpose. Deep, clear eyes, the velvet preview of future bearded cheek, your tempting lips, your gentle arms that would protect me from assault of weather and disdain.

BENVOLIO: All you have said, I say to you with twice the wonder. These arms, yearning, reach to you. Come, lace your fingers with mine.

MERCUTIO: Listen, Benvolio, there's music if you listen with your heart. Music that guides our steps. Do you hear?

(They dance.)

BENVOLIO: Hold me always. How sweet to touch your ear, your brow, your cheek.

MERCUTIO: To touch with fingers or with lips?

BENVOLIO: I had thought 'with fingers,' yet dream that lips may follow.

MERCUTIO: Fingers point the way; then lips must share their pleasure. Let all these holy places feel your moist implement of exploration.

BENVOLIO: What treasure exploration finds!

MERCUTIO: Come with your delicate fingers. Touch these lips you say you like, and they may like alike.

BENVOLIO: My lips had not thought to touch. Here is a dream, and I the dreamer.

MERCUTIO: Guide with your fingers my lips to where they may touch yours. See! When lips touch, eyes draw closed and imagination is invited to the fore.

BENVOLIO: Step back to the reach of my arms. Though I know you Mercutio, let me still see and touch my heart's desire. Never had I thought to have his kiss. Give me his kiss again!

MERCUTIO: His kiss? His kiss! Your kiss tells your love. Your lips tell who you love. He can be but Romeo.

BENVOLIO: Your guise uncovers mine. Affection I bear him as a friend has secretly been more. Now you know, pray seal your lips that have given this vicarious joy. Be friend to my passion.

(They embrace.)

MERCUTIO: I embrace your secret and yourself. As I am your friend and his, I will be friend to the secret of your love.

BENVOLIO: It is love, true, but harsh. You see where passion draws me, yet Romeo has eyes only for the fair sex. The stronger my passion, the more I must hold back. I yearn to tell but know I must not. There would be rejection, and friendship destroyed.

MERCUTIO: I think you trust too little. Knowing, am I no longer your friend? Truly, knowing I cherish our friendship the more. Surely Romeo loves you and learning of your love will love you still. Trust his friendship, I say. Friendships are ever buoyed in banishment of bedeviling secrets.

BENVOLIO: Logic is yours I'll grant, but this is a matter of emotions. I imagine telling but fear to tell.

MERCUTIO: I'll not say you must, yet in strength of friendship, friends may trust. Be happy there and confident.

BENVOLIO: My passion would be told but I fear to tell. Still, I'll think on all you've said. You have taught me much this night, great friend.

MERCUTIO: Until tomorrow then, when we shall learn what has transpired with Romeo.

BENVOLIO: Mercutio, farewell.

(They begin to exit separate ways.)

BENVOLIO: Hold, Mercutio. I would speak again. Tomorrow we will know Romeo's secret passions, and he shall know mine. You have the right of it. My passion will be happily confessed. As you bid, I'll trust in Romeo, our friendship still be blessed.

MERCUTIO: I say this friendship—his and yours—will be the stronger for it. Tomorrow will prove.

(They exit.)

74

Craig Martin

Craig's poetry has appeared in the *Northwest Gay & Lesbian Reader* and in *Koinos* Issue 68. His short story, "Broadway," appeared in *Gay City: Volume 2* where it was selected for an Editor's Choice Award. Among his current projects is a street-kid detective novel, Hard\Air. Craig has lived in Seattle not nearly long enough to be a native. For news of Benvolio's progress, email craig@craigtmartin.com. See more at www.craigtmartin.com and www.bmyguy.com.

THE DOCTOR IS IN

1952...

F. WERTHAM PSYCHIATRIST

"SHALL WE RESUME WHERE WE LEFT OFF, MR. WAYNE? TELL ME... ARE YOU STILL HAVING THOSE FANCIFUL DREAMS?"

I'D CALL THEM *NIGHTMARES*, REALLY, DOCTOR. I HAD ANOTHER LAST NIGHT.

PLEASE ELABORATE.

WELL, THIS ONE WAS THE MOST VIVID YET. IN THE DREAM I'M A *MILLIONAIRE* IN A MANSION. AND I HAVE A *YOUNG BOY* LIVING WITH ME.

IS THIS BOY A RELATIVE?

NO, NOT EXACTLY... HE'S MORE LIKE A WARD. HIS NAME IS *DICK.*

"DICK"? INTERESTING.

ME AND THE BOY LIKE TO DRESS UP IN COLORFUL UNDERWEAR.

UNDERWEAR?

MASKS?

AND WEAR MASKS.

AND ME AND THE BOY HAVE A SECRET ROOM UNDER THE HOUSE WHERE NO ONE CAN SEE WHAT WE DO. IT'S LIKE A CAVE.

UNDER THE HOUSE? HOW DO YOU GET THERE?

WE SLIDE ON BIG *POLES.*

I PUSH A SECRET BUTTON AND THE WALL OPENS UP LIKE A GIANT CLOSET WITH NO FLOOR, REVEALING A BIG, DARK HOLE TO THE CAVE. WE CLIMB ONTO THESE TWO BIG, SLIPPERY POLES AND RIDE THE SHINY SHAFTS DOWNWARD.

AND ON THE WAY TO THE CAVE ME AND THE BOY TAKE OUR CLOTHES OFF, PUT ON OUR MASKS AND CAPES AND UNDERWEAR AND WE'RE READY FOR ACTION.

"ACTION"? WHAT TYPE OF "ACTION"?

I'M NOT SURE EXACTLY...IT'S KIND OF FUZZY, BUT IN THE DREAM WE HAVE A LONG BLACK CAR AND WE'RE VERY EXCITED TO GET TO THE CITY WHERE SOME *STRANGE MEN* AWAIT US.

STRANGE HOW...?

WELL...THEY ALL WEAR WEIRD COSTUMES AND MASKS OR MAKEUP—

"MEN IN MAKEUP?!"

THERE'S A SHORT, FAT GUY IN A PERFECT TUXEDO AND TOP HAT WHO CARRIES AN UMBRELLA. AND THERE'S A GUY IN GREEN LEOTARDS WITH QUESTION MARKS ALL OVER IT. AND THE STRANGEST ONE OF ALL... A *QUEER* CLOWN IN *RAINBOW* COLORS—

RAINBOW?

AND LOTS OF PURPLE. HE HAS A WHITE FACE, BRIGHT GREEN HAIR AND BIG RED LIPS. HE'S ALWAYS LAUGHING AND DANCING AROUND.

SO...ARE THERE ANY *WOMEN* IN THESE DREAMS?

YES...ONE. SHE'S DRESSED AS A *SEXY CAT*—

SEXY CAT?

BUT I DON'T WANT ANYTHING TO DO WITH HER.

OH—

2

77

IT IS, OF COURSE, YOUR CHOICE, MR. WAYNE. YOU CAN ACCEPT YOUR *SICK, TORTURED, TWISTED* FUTURE OF A LIFE LIVED FOR *PENIS*...

..OR LET US HELP YOU BY REMOVING HALF YOUR BRAIN AND BEATING YOU INTO IRREPARABLE HUMILIATION WITH THE HOLY SCRIPTURES...

...SO THAT THE *MERE* THOUGHT OF ANOTHER MAN MAKES YOUR JOHN THOMAS RETREAT DEEPLY INTO YOUR LOWER INTESTINES.

THANK YOU SO MUCH, DR. WERTHAM, WITHOUT YOU I'D *NEVER* HAVE EVEN KNOWN I WAS A HOMOSEXUAL.

IT'S MY JOB TO HELP, MY BOY.

DON'T BE TOO HARD ON YOURSELF.

MOVIES, TELEVISION AND COMIC BOOKS ARE TURNING AMERICA INTO A COUNTRY OF UNBRIDLED *MAN-LOVING.*

I'VE MADE IT MY LIFE'S WORK TO REVEAL *SISSY-BOYS* WHEREVER THEY MAY HIDE AND, GOD-WILLING, HEAL THE AFFLICTION.

WOW- I DIDN'T EVEN KNOW I WAS *AFFLICTED!!*

I CAN *SMELL* A HOMOSEXUAL A MILE AWAY, MR. WAYNE. REMEMBER- I'M A *DOCTOR!*

AH, MISS. PRINCE, PLEASE COME IN.

THANK YOU, DOCTOR WERTHAM.

TELL ME, ARE YOU STILL HAVING THOSE DREAMS?

THEY'RE EVEN MORE VIVID, DOCTOR.

IN THEM, I'M A STRONG *AMAZONIAN* WOMAN *WARRIOR* LIVING ON AN ISLAND WITH NO MEN ALLOWED.

HMMM, TELL ME DIANA, WHEN DID YOU FIRST REALIZE YOU WERE A *LESBIAN?*

END

STORY AND ART COPYRIGHT 2011 STEVE GOUPIL

82

Steven Goupil

Steven's character, Dickie Derringer, previously appeared in *Gay City: Volume 3*. Steven is currently working on several LGBT projects and creating a website (gayity.com) around his and other's LGBT art work to be up next year. He is also working on other comics, humor and romance pieces and hopes to continue to do so for many years.

Pirate Games

Evan J. Peterson

I did light out for that Territory and I had me a time. Jim left to find work and buy up his wife and kids, and I lived with Widow Douglas for what seemed like the whole winter through to spring before I'd had enough of schooling and stiff clothes and bibles and such. Soon as it was warm enough, I got Judge Thatcher to give me enough of my treasure money to get across the river on a ferry. I had to slip away in the early morning, and so's not to worry the Widow and Miss Watson I left them a real long fancy note as follows:

Dear Ladies, I thank you kindly for all the sivilizing you've done me, feeding and schooling and whatnot. You are mighty good women and I'm sure you'll go to that Good Place yet, but not too soon, since I don't wish either you to die before you are ready. I must light out for the Territory beyond the Missasippi to seek my fortune amongst the unspoilt country of our great land, god bless America, and so on and so forth. Do not cry for my lost youth etsetra. I will come back and visit I promise. Your humble boy Huck Finn.

On the boat I met an old man and he talked to me about the river like old folks do. I think if people would listen to old folks more often, they would prolly have less to say.

He tells me, "This virgin river divides a child America from an adult America."

I asked him what virgin was, and he says it's a girl who ain't married. I wondered what that had to do with a river, but old folks get notions that nobody but their like can explain.

"Just girls?" I ask him, and he says yes, that there's something that changes in a girl when she's married that doesn't change for a boy. I don't know what he meant, but I reckon it has to do with babies. I heard Miss Watson and Widow Douglas talking one time about a girl in town, talking real low and quiet-like about this girl who was going to have a baby, and hoping Jesus would take it to the Good Place, and not two days later that girl got married. I done a lot of growing up on this river, and I guess if the river is a girl then maybe she's my Ma, tho my mama had me and some other babies that died so maybe the river isn't a virgin after all.

I don't remember Ma too well, but I remember her singing songs to me that made me feel like everything was alright and nothing could hurt me, and that's how the river always makes me feel. I nearly died more times'n I can count on this river, but I always make it out alive. Maybe Ma's ghost lives in there, keeping me safe and watching me grow up. Maybe she drowned right here in the Missasippi like I nearly done time and again. Pap never let me talk much about my Ma to other people, since she was half injun and all, why I'm so much browner than Tom and Joe and near everybody.

So, nothin' to lose, I rode that boat across, and I didn't feel no different on the other side 'cept for thinking to myself, this is it Huck, you're on your own. When I was hungry, I fished or ate berries and such. I was used to sleeping in hog sheds and the like, so finding a comfortable place to sleep warn't too difficult. I met all kinds of people, fur trappers and injuns, but I didn't stay long in one place. I never been much good with time, but I reckon I was by myself near six months, since it got hot and started to get cool again. Then I started to worry. I didn't know how far north or south or west I was, hadn't really cared enough to ask nobody, and I didn't know if it would get real bitter cold or not.

Just my luck, I found a village, and I was afeared at first that they'd kill me, but then I thought maybe if I told them my mother was half injun they'd take me in. I walked into that village with my hands up, waving my white shirt in surrender, tho it warn't too white no more, and they captured me real quick. Come to find out some of them spoke English from trading with trappers, tho more of them spoke French. I told them that my Ma was like them, and they couldn't kill just half or a quarter of me, and then I gave them my pipe and some tobacco and they took me in.

I seen some mighty odd things in that village, all kinds of magic and whatnot. I seen a ghost get pulled right out a man's belly by another man who dressed like a woman. He wore woman's clothes every day, and not cause he was playing a trick. They called him Two Spirits and didn't think a thing about it. I lived with them five winters, got to speak their language, even had me a blood brother like Tom was, but that's a story for another day. This is a story about what happens on the river.

Nice as they was to me, and much as I loved my blood brother, I got powerful homesick and had to light out for home again. Next time they made their way to the river to trade, they took me with them. I worked extra hard to get enough fur and whatnot to trade for enough money to get back to the other side of the river.

Sure as you're born, it didn't take but a day to get back to town. I strutted into town with my tribe clothes on, and folks just about dropped dead. Widow Douglas was so happy to see me she near cried, tho Miss Watson didn't trust me on account I'd been injunized, as she called it. The widow told me I'd grown into such a man, and she fetched some of them stiff clothes for me to wear, but I told her since I was a man now that if I was going to wear white man's clothing again then it better not be too itchy and stiff. She found an old shirt and some britches that her husband used to wear, and tho they weren't as comfortable as my tribe clothes they'd do.

Tell you what, soon as I got into them fancy old clothes, there was a knock at the door and who do you reckon it was but Tom Sawyer, my first and dearest blood brother, all grown up like a carrot. He was so happy to see me he clapped me on the back like I was an eraser at the school. I hadn't even thought about an eraser in years, and I wondered if they'd make me sit and read books again. That got me to thinking how I needed to make this visit a quick one.

I got to telling Tom all about the tribe, and my blood brother, and the fur trapping. So long had gone by. Tom was all of seventeen, and I— well, I never been sure how old I am. Taller'n Tom, that's sure. He asked me a hundred and one questions, until it was so late that the Widow told Tom he'd have to go home. The next day being Saturday, and Tom not having anything to do, we agreed to go down to Jackson's Island to go fishing.

Soon as we got down there, all by ourselves, I took off them clothes, but I folded them up real nice since they must'a been special to the Widow, having belonged to her dead husband and all. I learned a lot of respect in my time with that tribe. Tom stripped off too, and we ran right into the water and splashed around a long time.

"You smell just awful, Huck! What do they feed you in that village?" He grabbed me and tried to rub water on my underarms, but I wiggled away. I ducked him under, but I knew he was just picking at me. Jealous, prolly, that I get to be a real explorer and he can only play pretend. I bet if he could he'd smell like this too.

I spent that whole summer camping on Jackson's Island. Seemed like I spent more time there than at the Widow's house, which I guess suited her and her sister just as well. Tom came down less often, having to do work to keep up his aunt's place. He became real close with Joe Harper, and brought Joe with him sometimes, though other times he said Joe couldn't make it. He was lying at least once I knew because when they got down to the island Joe was real quiet and I could tell he was sore about something. He mentioned later that Tom should'a told him last time he was coming down, that he had spent all day inside from the rain. It kinda made me feel good, knowing that Tom would rather see me and just me sometimes. I guess I know how Joe felt too cause sometimes Tom would go off with Joe and not invite me along. I got to wondering why I wasn't invited, but I figgered it was one'a Tom's little games, makin' me and Joe Harper jealous of each other like that.

One day, Tom was down on the island with me, and we were being real lazy and lying around in the shade. Out of nowheres, Tom says, "Do you miss Jim?" and I reckon I did and missed him something mighty. I told Tom as much, and I got to thinking about old Jim and me on Jackson's Island, on the raft. Jim would always call me Honey and I reckon that's what black folk say when they care about somebody. Not many people ever cared about me more'n a hill of beans.

I remember lying on that raft in the sunshine, not a care in the world, us both just naked as the day we were born. All these stiff clothes that Tom's 'spected to wear, well I don't reckon I know how he can stand it sometimes. Ain't natural if you ask me, and I told him as much.

Tom says to me, "What was that like, being naked with a full grown man?" I told him there warn't nothing to it. Hot out, you're on a raft, you don't wear no clothes. 'Sides, I told Tom, we been running around the island naked since we was little, and now we're grown and we're still naked, what's the difference? He kinda turned away from me then, bashful I reckon, not wanting me to see his boy parts. But Tom's funny like that, 'specially since I come back and we both got hair under our arms and on our boy parts and whatnot, sometimes he's okay with me seeing him and sometimes not. I was sitting there wondering to myself, don't Tom know me better'n that? Then Tom says to me the oddest thing I ever heard him say, and believe me he says some odd things.

He says, "Anything pick-yoo-lee-er happen when you two was naked on the raft?" Says it just like that, pick-yoo-lee-er.

"Like what, Tom?" I says, starting to get fed up, "Confound you, you're talkin' all around something in that head a' yours. What kinda notion you got?" He was worrying the ground with some stick he had. Then out'a nowheres, he says, "Didn't you never, you know... try touching Jim?"

That was about all I could take'a his questions. All his book learning, and he's asking me about things I barely even thought about, 'specting me to have done this and that and played some kinda naked touching game with my friend. I picked up a half a handful of sand and threw it at him.

Well, Tom and I got into a big fuss, he punched me in the shoulder and I knocked him one, but Tom's always been a dirty fighter and knocks my legs out from under me. I'm not down that easy, and I grabbed him and we tumped over the tree roots. This point, Tom was on top'a me, and started laughing and looking at me funny. My back hurt on the ground and Tom's weight was pushing me into the roots, but I didn't move.

"Say you're sorry, Tom," I says to him.

"For what?" he says, holding me down by the shoulders. He had his knees on my legs in a way that kept me from getting a good foot to lift up.

"For asking me if I was touching Jim! What does that even mean? It can't be nothing good, knowing you and your mind!" I says. I was thinking about spitting in his eye, but maybe that wouldn't a' been fair. Even if Tom fights dirty, I know well and good to fight fair.

Sometimes I get afraid that Tom'll go too far, and then I'll go too far, and Tom'll get sore about it and stop being my friend. Pain in the britches that Tom is, I'd go to Hell or even church for him. 'Sides, I guess I deserved being down there with my back against them rough roots for throwing the sand at him.

88

"You say it, Huck," Tom says. I tried to raise up but Tom had me. "Say sorry."

"I'm sorry, Tom, now get off'a me!" He did, that rat, and as he flipped over I saw his boy parts had gotten big. He kinda shut his legs together and turned his body so I couldn't see, but I seen it already. That got me to thinking about what he'd said.

A lot of moments went by and we didn't say nothin'. He was breathin' hard, lookin' all around but not at me. Then I asked him what he meant by touching. He says I know just what he means. Like you touch yourself sometimes. I says to Tom, "I ain't never touched Jim like that."

"Funny," Tom says, and starts laughing his little fake laugh when I can tell he's got something cooking in his brain like a fever. Not like how he was laughing when he had me on the ground. The kinda laugh that the Widow Douglas would call, "downright sinister."

"What's so funny," I ask him, but he keeps right on with his little snickering. He was still sitting with his body turned away from me. After a moment he says to me, "So you wouldn't touch Jim like that, huh?" and he took a long time to say Jim's name, like when he said pick-yoooo-lier.

"Damn right I wouldn't. I'd feel mighty rotten touchin' Jim like that. That's for a man to do by hisself." Then Tom says something that changes things, and I mean changes them forever. Made me feel like I'd just spent a year on that river, learned so much in a moment.

"It ain't for a man to do alone, neither."

I could feel my heart beating hard, and not because I'd just wrestled Tom. I'd been touching myself time to time, most days seemed like, but never with anyone around. Just didn't seem proper to do somethin' with my privates in front'a someone else. I knowed Tom did it too, we talked about it once, but I ain't never heard tell of men or boys doing that together.

Not hearing back from me, Tom kept right on talking. "I done it with another boy before." Then I couldn't help wondering out loud. "Who, Tom?"

"Nobody," he says. He moved, sitting with his back to one tree, across from me, my back to the other tree. I remember hearing the morning dove calling then. To me it always sounded like, "Who cooks for who?"

Tom looked at me with one eye, and tho his face was turned to the side I could tell he was smiling with only half his mouth.

"I bet it was Ben Rogers," I says, "fool that he is. He'd let you sell him a wooden nickel."

"Wasn't neither," he says.

"Then it has to be Joe Harper. Did you touch Joe's parts, Tom?" I was curious, and kinda worried, and a little of something else all at once.

"Never you mind, Huck. Ain't your concern."

"Why'd you bring it up, then? Secrets are for girls, Tom!"

Tom looked full at me then. I didn't know what to do. I could feel my blood all hot in my face, and then I started to feel it hot all over.

"You wanna watch me, Huck? We could both do it. Ain't no shame to it." I didn't say nothing, just looked down at my body and my own parts.

"This is our place, Huck. Nobody's gonna see. Ain't no steamboat floating loaves of bread full of quicksilver and people after it." He made me laugh then. He came over and sat next to me. There I was on Jackson's Island, in the place that I could get away from everyone, even Tom most times, and I was sitting with my back on a tree, the big bumpy old roots under my legs kinda hurting me, but in a good way, you know, like when you get whupped for something and you know you deserve it, and there was Tom, looking at me. I was still wondering who else he'd done this with. Sure as you're born, I bet it was Joe Harper.

Tom brushed the sand off his hands real well, and I did it too, so's not to get them little bits on my tenderest parts. Tom started in on himself, I started in on myself, and it felt good, good as it ever did, but new, too. Tough to put it in words. It was just like doing it regular, but like doing it in a dream, where it's familiar but also not, all at once. I guess mostly I was just surprised at myself doing this with Tom, but I didn't want him to get mad at me or feel all embarrassed about bringing it up. It didn't really feel too strange once we'd started, tho I was still feeling nervous.

Then Tom says, "You're doing it wrong."

I says to him, "I always do it like this."

Tom says, "No, watch me," and he kinda rubs himself with his whole hand instead of the way I do it using the skin at the end. Then he turns his hand upside down and does the same thing backward. I tried to do it like that, but it was just strange and I wanted to do it my way, so I did.

He says, "Stop, Huck, do it the right way."

I says, "I like my way," and I almost threw more sand on him but thought that he would wrestle me again, and that might be just what he wanted.

"You don't know anything, Huck. You'll break it like that, the way you're doin it. It'll make your hands hairy if you do that."

"I ain't broke it yet, and I got as much hair on the back of my hands as you do."

"Look, there's a right way and a wrong way."

"Oh yeah? Who showed you the right way? Joe? Or did you read it in one a' them fancy books? The Big Book Of How To Touch Your Boy Parts? I knowed you ain't read about this in no bible."

I stopped then. Tom stopped too, and he says, "Why you keep bringin' up Joe for? You jealous or somethin'?"

I got real huffy then and stood up. Tom was still sitting against the tree but I could see that look in his eye like he was up to something. "Nothin' to be jealous about, Tom! You think jest cause you been doin' this with another boy and not me that I'm jealous? I was doin' this fine on my own till you decided to show me your damn fool 'right way'!"

Tom stood up then, and caught me by the arm and tried to get me to sit down again, but I warn't ready to do that. I was mad at him, and he was gonna hear about it. I told him to quit, but he wouldn't let go, so I went for his legs like he did with mine before, and I knocked him down but he took me with him, that rat, and we tumbled in the grass until he was on top of me again. For some reason, all I could think was how we used to do this all the time when we were kids, and it was just different now, wouldn't be like that ever again, not ever.

He was looking right into me, like my face was a few inches back from its rightful place, like he was looking into eyes that were inside my head 'stead of out. Then I starts thinking the strangest thing yet, pick-yoo-lee-er alright. I starts to feel like I belonged there, under him I mean. It felt good. I know it sounds crazy, but it felt good having Tom pin me down like that, his knees on my legs and his hands holding my wrists against the sand and grass. Who feels good being held down like that? Maybe Joe Harper.

"There's a right way and a wrong way, Huck. Now you gotta tell me to stop but not stop me." Confound that Tom Sawyer.

"What am I supposed to say?"

"You're supposed to beg me not to do nothing to you, but then you don't stop me, neither. That's the way of it."

I looked up at him and his body was so pink, not like mine. "If I don't want you to stop, why I got to tell you to?"

"It's just the way it's done, Huck. Pirates do this to each other all the time. I read about it in one of Judge Thatcher's law books. That's when there ain't no women around. Then, when they sack a village and they kidnap the women, they do this to them. The pirates do it to each other while they're out at sea, but some of them act like the women so the others can practice."

"But women ain't got no boy parts, Tom."

Tom's eyes got really wide then, and he starts laughing fit to raise the dead and drops on top a' me. I let him be there. It felt good, his body pressing mine into the grass like that, his skin against mine. I raised my hands above my head and I told him okay, he could pin me again.

He did, and he brushed his free hand off real slow on my side, and it kinda tickled but not in a bad way. I told him to cut it out, that it warn't right what he was doing to me, that I'd tell the authorities, and other stuff I'd heard that sounded like what you say when someone's got you pinned down touching you nasty and won't let you up. Damn foolish, if you ask me, but that's what Tom wanted and I guess I didn't really want him to let up on me just yet.

"See Huck, when you touch yourself, you gotta do it like this," and then he starts in on me. I reckon it did feel better than what I do, but I think it was probably just that he was doing it and not me, like how you can't really tickle your own self. There was so much going on, his left hand pushing my wrists into the grass, his right hand working on me, his knees kinda hurting the thickest parts of my legs, his toes wiggling against my knees. It's like I got lost in my own body.

He did that until the special thing happened that always happens if you do it long enough. We went into the water and got cleaned up then, and when we got back to the trees he wanted me to do the same thing to him, but not pin him down. He said he was the captain and I was the mate, and the mate doesn't push the captain down. Sometimes he sounds like he's making sense but then I think on what he tells me, and it don't really.

So he sat down against the tree and I sat in front of him and tried to do what he'd done on me, and he got to the end part a lot quicker than I had. It got on me, and I ran into the water quick like a rabbit.

Seems like each time we went back there to Jackson's Island that summer, he had something new he wanted to show me. Most of it was nice, but some things took all day to convince me to do. Usually he'd get me to agree to let him do something to me, and then when I knew it warn't nothing to be scared of, I'd do it to him too. Some days he just wanted me to do everything and him not do anything back. When I'd flat out refuse, cause that ain't fair, he'd wrestle me down and pin me again and I'd pretend I was saying no. That got him real excited, and I never did understand what that was all about. Take it or leave it, I don't see why nobody needs to play pretend games just to touch each other.

One day, soon as we got to the island, I started taking off my britches, and Tom says, "No, I don't want to do that no more."

"Why not?" I says, real confused. I thought playing pirates was Tom's favorite.

"Because I turned eighteen already, and that's how old you are when you stop doing that with other boys."

"What about me? I don't even know how old I am, so that means I can do it however much I want." I'd started liking it more and more, and wondering about doing it with other boys 'sides Tom. Girls, too. It must be real different with a girl, and I mean to try it.

"Well," says Tom, "I heard that what we been doing is supposed to be something a man does with a woman only."

"Read that in a book, did you?" I asked him, meaner than I should'a been. He looked at me and he warn't even angry, just looking mighty sad. It hurt me to see that, so I told him I was sorry. "I thought that's what pirates did, Tom. When women weren't around."

"I'm gettin' too old to play pirate games, Huck."

That made me sad too. Tom's always been my captain. This whole touching thing we'd been up to, it really was like being pirates, adventuring on them high seas. Like we were discovering treasure and new islands. His hands were the gold on Cuba, his mouth was rubies on Jamayka, and I always thought that special part at the end was the pearls, for obvious reasons, etsetra.

That day we didn't talk much. I got him to play pirates one more time after the sun set, and did whatever he wanted me to do, even that one thing he really likes but I don't like because it kinda hurts, but that was the last time he went to Jackson's Island with me. I still see Tom around, but it ain't the same. He's gonna marry Becky Thatcher, and then she'll have babies and she won't be a virgin no more. I reckon I'll go back across that river to the tribe, where I can show them everything I learned this summer. Lately, I gone back to touching alone, and it ain't the same. It's not even the touching I miss so much. I miss Tom. It was his idea to start it all, and it's just foolish that he can't look me in the eye no more. It's just not natural to give up your blood brother like that.

Evan J. Peterson

lives and writes in Seattle, where he teaches writing classes for several organizations. He publishes poetry, fiction, and nonfiction and reviews books for TheRumpus.net. Recent and forthcoming work can be found in *Weird Tales*, Sweetlit.com, *Court Green, Assaracus,* and *Aim For The Head: An Anthology Of Zombie Poetry.* He is the founding editor of *ZiReZi,* the zine review zine from Seattle's Zine Archive & Publishing Project.

My Craft

Louis Flint Ceci

"The solution, I should think, is obvious," I said, setting aside my glass of sherry. "They are your rooms, not his. You must ask him to leave."

My brother winced. "I've grown rather attached to him." I raised an eyebrow but he dismissed it with an impatient wave of his hand. "I find him stimulating, but not in that way."

"If not in that way, then in what way? Why does he hang about so? Why is he as often found in your rooms as his own? What draws him to you if not the perception that you are drawn to him?"

"I assure you I take the greatest pains to display no emotion whatsoever in his presence."

"An absence of evidence is evidence in itself. You yourself have said so. Besides, if you were truly as disinterested as you claim, then his whereabouts and where-with-all would be of no concern. Send him packing."

"Now you're merely being glib. His case is more complex than that."

"How so?"

"If you had seen the state he was in when he returned from India . . ."

I raised my hand to stop him. "Do not fill me with sentimental nonsense about his being a wounded war veteran. I shan't have it."

"No, it isn't that." He unwound his lanky frame from the chair and glanced around the room. There was no one else within earshot, but even if there were, the members of my Club would be too discreet (or too deaf) to listen. "You are correct in your methods," he said, "but not in your conclusion." He began pacing before the fireplace. "He has a mind that is in constant turmoil, seeking to find some object to which it may become affixed, some unexplained phenomenon which appears, on its surface, inconceivably complex or contradictory, but which, at its heart, has a simple, rational explanation."

"Hence his profession."

"Precisely! Furthermore, this outward focus keeps him from turning inward, to the turmoil and—so he imagines—disgust he would find there."

"And why should he find that?"

He raised his eyes to the ceiling and flung wide his arms. "The signs are all there! His early athleticism, his enlisting in that foolish Afghan adventure, his incessant womanizing. You know the pattern."

People mistake my slowness to anger for patience or indifference. It is neither. It is the conviction that anger is wasted on the foolish. However, that conviction was sorely tested by my brother's condescension. I picked up my sherry. "We all face that turmoil and disgust. You have reached your accommodation with it, as have I. The good doctor must find his own."

"You do not understand. I feel if he were to discover the actual truth about himself, it would destroy him."

He stared at me but I refused to let him pull me along in this melodramatic fashion. "I can well understand how such self-knowledge might destroy a man—if he were weak to begin with—but that is not my problem, and it is not yours."

He stopped for a moment, his hand caught in the tangle of his hair. Then his shoulders slumped and he let out a sigh. "You are quite right. I shall simply have to ask him to go."

My brother can be uncommonly thick at times. I saw that, despite all my efforts, I should have to lead him step by step to the proper course of action. "Don't be an idiot. The problem is not whether he is weak or not, but whether he is as strongly driven to avoid inner scrutiny as you say."

"But what am I to do?" He resumed pacing. "I cannot let him stay or he will surely stumble upon—"

I cut him off. "I do not wish to hear what he might stumble upon. Whatever arrangement you have with Lastrade is your own affair and I wish to hear none of the details."

"And yet you say, contradicting your first position, that neither can I send him packing."

I rose from my chair, which silenced him and stilled his nervous activity. As calmly as I could, I said, "If you ask him to go, that will only provoke his curiosity. He may be incapable of discovering himself, but he's perfectly capable of discovering you. And Lastrade. And worse, me. The boats to France are full enough as it is. I will not have this tiresome army surgeon, decorated or not, filling them further."

"Then he must never discover it." The color drained from his face. "Surely, you are not suggesting—?"

I walked to the mullioned window and stared at the bare trees in the courtyard below. "No." I turned to face him. "You say his mind needs a point of fixation? Then we shall fix it. Does he like to write?"

"Yes. Constantly scribbling in that damned notebook of his."

"Then we shall give him something to write about. I know enough actors and other lay-abouts to fill ten theatres. It will not be hard to supply them with props."

Dawn rose in his face again and a disgustingly boyish smile crept across it. "You mean—?"

"Precisely. The doctor wants mysteries. We'll give him mysteries. He may even pretend to solve them."

"Ah, hmmm, . . . " my brother hesitated.

I sighed. Why must the younger sibling always have the larger ego? "Very well, then, you may solve them. But he must be so engaged he will notice nothing else, nothing but the game."

"Which he will never guess truly is a game!"

"You have a talent, brother mine, for declaring the elementary."

That very afternoon we drew up a series of intricate conundrums. Constructing the elaborate ruses became a most engaging pastime. Over time, it grew from a mere expediency into a sort of elegant machinery. Not as intricate as architecture nor as profound as mathematics, but satisfying all the same. A craft, you might say. And it worked, as I knew it would, perfectly. Moreover, after the doctor published his first few accounts, we soon had many collaborators, both in London and on the Continent. The game was even sufficiently intriguing to cause me to stir from my Club on one or two occasions to stand in for the supposed arch-villain pulling the strings behind the scenes.

There were a few close calls and complications, of course. Once or twice, we stumbled upon actual crimes, some of which seemed to have been inspired by the very webs we ourselves had woven. Lastrade's star rose within the Force, but how that affected his relationship with my brother I did not care to ask. I should imagine, however, that it involved some alteration in their usual costumes.

My one disappointment with the whole business was in the titles the good doctor concocted for his "adventures." Many were unduly sensationalized and some downright inaccurate. I will not bother to correct the record, for really, once one starts, where can one end? My sole consolation is that he never did finish his chronicle of our finest confabulation, "The Giant Rat of Sumatra," perhaps as it skated too close to the mark. As he remains silent on the matter, so shall I—save to mention that, in truth, he was no rat, and frankly, I had seen larger.

Louis Flint Ceci

has published poems in *Colorado North Review*; short stories and essays in *Diseased Pariah News*; articles on linguistics and poetics in College English; and an autobiographical essay in *Queer and Catholic*, edited by Amie M. Evans and Trebor Healey (Routledge, 2008). *Comfort Me*, his first novel, was published in 2008 by Prizm Books. He is an avid swimmer and medaled most recently at the 2nd AsiaPacific Outgames in Wellington, New Zealand.

Harry and the Forgotten Fuckbuddy

Ryan Crawford

His spine shivered and shook under wet, white skin. He convulsed on the frost-covered ground among dead leaves and patches of frozen snow. Ron watched him struggle for breath through gritted teeth, sure that the air was sharp and cold as Harry inhaled. Steam puffed from his mouth arrhythmically. Ron was freezing too, his soaked clothes clinging to him like an icy second skin. But it didn't seem to matter just now.

Ron found him.

There was a thick red ring of raw scrapes where the locket chain had strangled Harry's neck. He clutched himself against the cold, naked. Finally catching his breath, Harry turned to face Ron. His eyes widened in shock. Ron strained his chattering jaw to finally get the words out.

"W-why—the—*hell*," he pushed through the shudders, still gripping the locket chain and the sword he used to sever it, "d-didn't you t-take this—off—b-before you d-dived?"

Harry sat silent and quaking. He didn't take his eyes off Ron's.

The sword made a soft thud in the snow as Ron dropped it to kneel to Harry. He reached for Harry's clothes on the ground and, though shivering himself, forced the dry sweater over Harry's bare arms and chest. If Ron's fingers hadn't been numb from the cold, he imagined Harry's thighs would have felt glacial as he helped him into his pants and coat.

He wrapped his arms around Harry from behind (telling himself it was for the body heat) and tried not to say anything when Harry's hands found his. Harry's grip was fiercely strong, and Ron felt on the verge of tears. All these months alone, but he was welcomed back now.

Then Harry punched him. Hard.

"W-where the fuck have you been!?" Harry roared.

Ron sat sprawled on the ground by the frozen pond from which he just fucking *saved* Harry, rubbing his cheek. "Fuck was that for?" he sputtered. Weren't they just embracing?

"You left us! Me and Hermione! You were supposed to help us find the rest of them! You said you'd help me destroy them, so I can destroy him! And then you…" he trailed off, massaging the knuckles that just struck Ron's face, "… you… bloody *ran away*!"

The cold was nothing compared to the hot guilt that now oozed its way through Ron's veins.

"I know, mate."

"Lousy git!"

"I know."

"Son of a bitch!"

"Hey!" Ron shouted. "Don't talk about my mum! I came back, didn't I?"

Harry stormed around the edge of the frozen pond. The iced surface was broken where Harry dived, presumably for that goddamned sword, into subzero water where a possessed locket managed to nearly drown him. Fucking idiot.

The locket they had taken turns wearing that autumn (before Ron had left, as Harry was keen to point out) was no ordinary necklace. It harbored a piece of the soul belonging to the most powerful Dark wizard in history. Ron never said the name, always "You-Know-Who" as every sane witch and wizard would do, unlike Harry, and lately Hermione. They were both fairly ballsy when it came to facing this enemy. Maybe that was why the locket hadn't affected them as much when they'd worn it. Not like it had Ron.

It started out alright enough. They knew they couldn't return to school after all the disappearances and murders began. Ron dropped out to go with Harry. They'd have a lot more of You-Know-Who's artifacts to find, more fragments of his soul to vanquish, before he would finally be mortal and beaten. They'd all left together, Ron tagging along, disappearing and reappearing here and there, anywhere Hermione could think of, in hopes of evading You-Know-Who's forces. But as the days trudged on, the conversations between the three of them became sparser. The locket grew heavier and heavier on Ron's neck, weighing him down with contempt. Harry's touch became rarer. Hermione's hands strayed more frequently over Harry's ever-tensing shoulders.

Yeah, he ran away. Ron had chucked the locket at their feet and left Harry to prove yet again how he, Harry, could stand it up for a girl. He seemed to have a talent for stringing Ron along like a devoted puppy, only to turn him away when people started talking at school. *Spend an awful lot of time together, don't you?* They'd say. *Never seem to leave the bloke alone. You sure you're not polishing Harry's broomstick, Ron?*

They were best friends. More than that, Ron was Harry's *first* friend. He'd offered Harry a seat on the train when they were eleven, off to their first year at school. To be honest, Ron was unnerved at first at how damn clingy this skinny little kid was, shaggy-haired and not a clue about his own wizard heritage. But he was an orphan, parents killed by You-Know-Who. Ron's mum told him to keep an eye out for the Boy Who Lived. So he took him under his wing, showed him the ropes.

Little pipsqueak Harry, famous before he even knew about magic, turned out to be a real show off. During their first year of school: foiled You-Know-Who's first attempt to get a body back. Year two: got a tip off from a great bloody big spider, spoke to a giant fucking snake, then killed said giant fucking snake with the sword that now rested on the snow by Ron's wet feet. In the years after that, Harry battled his parents' betrayer, survived You-Know-Who's second attempt at murdering him, survived You-Know-Who's third and fourth attempts at murdering him, and then learned he would need to murder You-Know-Who himself. There were casualties along the way. Harry's competitor, Harry's godfather, and most recently, the school headmaster Professor Dumbledore, the one person alive whom You-Know-Who feared. And Harry was always there. The only things that followed Harry as much as Ron and Hermione did were the rumors, the reverence, the fame.

It was a good day when someone could remember Ron's name.

"Why did you come back?" Harry asked through chattering teeth.

Of course this question would be his next. Even still, Ron couldn't quite pinpoint the answer. Devoted friendship? Unconditional love? Maybe, but the real answers stemmed more from loneliness, horniness, and making damn well sure Hermione kept her hands off Ron's man.

"Knew you'd need me to come along and rescue you from murderous jewelry, I expect."

Harry winced a smile. It was easier this way.

A long time passed there in the dark Forest of Dean, the two of them silently drying off with their wands while the trees rustled above with a biting breeze. Ron thought of what things would have been like if You-Know-Who hadn't ever been born. His sister would never have been taken advantage of by You-Know-Who's possessed journal, his father wouldn't have been nearly killed by a giant fucking snake (different kind, this one), his oldest brother wouldn't have been scarred by a werewolf, and another brother, one of the twins, wouldn't be missing an ear. Of course, even with You-Know-Who around and rising to power again, he still might not have done these things to Ron's family had they not been so bent on protecting Harry. It would have been more convenient if another foster family had stepped up as his bodyguards. He was allegedly the Chosen One, this Boy Who Lived, alone destined to bring an end to it all; Harry, who brought about You-Know-Who's first downfall with his *forehead*. He'd only been a baby then. And Harry had about as much of an idea how to defeat You-Know-Who now as he did the first time.

Encouraging.

Still, Harry was Ron's best mate. And first love. He showed Ron unparalleled loyalty and kindness (at least, as much as can be expected from a teenaged boy with a hero complex). He had defended Ron's family, famously poor and overcrowded with children. To everyone else it seemed they had exactly opposite lives, Ron having the family Harry was robbed of, Harry born into fame and fortune and talent that Ron envied and admired. Though their histories were woven so differently, their presents were braided together in three cords: friendship, a mission to defeat You-Know-Who, and a yearning so deep that Ron dare not speak it out loud.

Suddenly a noise cut the silence. Harry and Ron looked around to see what might be lurking in the thicket around them but nothing surfaced. Only after the noise repeated, a kind of rapid clicking like an insect would make, did Ron realize it was coming from his hand.

He opened his fingers and looked at the gold and emerald trinket in his palm. It was as if the locket was calling to him, pleading even. Ron abruptly felt a wave of defensiveness for it, like it was his duty to protect it from harm.

Harry approached slowly. "Ron," he said.

Ron kept his eyes on the locket. It kept clicking as if to say something to him.

"Ron, you were the one who pulled the sword from the lake."

The clicking was pitiful, like a whimper, like the cry of a forgotten little boy.

"You're the one who must destroy it. "

Ron watched as his fingers wrapped themselves over the glinting golden surface of the locket. The clicking was muffled by his closing fist. "I don't think I can, mate. It's like… it's like I can't hurt it."

"Then set it down," Harry said. "Just there. Drop it on the ground."

It felt like a herculean effort to simply open his fingers and let the pendant and severed chain slip through his grasp (did he only imagine that the chain tried to coil itself around his thumb?) and fall to the snow below. The locket rattled louder now. It was afraid, or angry.

"Use the sword, Ron." Harry looked ready to pounce, whether on the locket, on the sword, or even on Ron himself to make sure he followed through. "I'll open it, and then you strike."

Ron ceremoniously raised the heavy sword over his head, ready to bring down the blow. Harry pulled out what looked like Hermione's wand (where was his own?) and pointed it at the locket.

"On the count of three," Harry announced. "One."

Ron tightened his grip on the sword's ruby-encrusted handle. The sun was beginning to rise.

"Two!"

He felt a sting in his armpits and butterflies in his stomach. Could he do this?

"THREE!"

Ron didn't know what happened. There was the sound of hissing (Harry's snake language that always seemed to be a prelude to a really awful situation), a small flicker of light, the sound of a metal clink, then Ron was lifted from his feet and thrown back onto the ground in a great explosion of black.

There was nothing but sound and cold then. Ron knew he was in the snow. The sword was somewhere to his right. A roaring beat down on him as if caught in a dark storm.

A voice called. *Harry!* Ron thought. But the voice was frigid and brittle like the ice of the frozen pond, not deep and warm like Harry's became after their fourth year at school.

Don't embarrass yourself, the voice hissed. Somehow it sounded like it was coming from within Ron's own head than from the rising, swirling mass of black smoke twisting from the open locket like a tornado, thick as a thunderhead. *You haven't the strength.*

Ron couldn't speak. He watched as the black fog seemed to congeal and sink lower to the ground. Shapes began to form around it. Long, spindly shapes from its edges…

I have seen into your heart, Ronald. The voice made the red hairs on the back of his freckled neck stand up. The spindly shapes touched to the ground, eight of them. *And frankly honey, I wasn't impressed.*

Ron felt his jaw drop. What did this thing just say? And why did it sound suddenly like RuPaul?

Look at you. Look at you! A penniless queer ginger who has nothing better to do than risk his fucking neck for a twink with a death wish and glasses two sizes too small? Ron. Ron, Ron, Ron. Get a goddamn grip!

The spindly shapes that Ron feared would turn into enormous spider legs merely swirled back toward the great cyclone in the center.

"Who—who are you? How do you know my name?" Ron croaked, his voice shaken with surprise.

Bitch you've only been WEARING me for the past few months! You get to know a guy after being strung along that long. The cyclone writhed, and for a moment Ron saw Harry on the other side. It looked as if he was trying to get up from the ground.

And SPEAKING of being strung along, let's just recap your pathetic crush on this 'Chosen One' trick. The twister seemed to curve a bit, as if it was jutting out a hip. *Baby, you were always going to fall for him. He's popular, he's mysterious, he's strong, he's subtle… in a word, everything you're not.*

"I don't know what you're talking about!" Ron shouted. He looked for the sword. Where had he dropped it?

Let's not, shall we? I may be a piece of an evil man's soul trapped in a locket for some odd years and a little hot to trot with my debut, but I wasn't born under a rock. You're in love with him.

"Don't be ridiculous!" Ron yelled, though the force he'd been going for was pointless when his voice cracked on the last word.

What's 'ridiculous' is your pathology, hunty. Last son born to a mother who had already delivered FIVE boys? Have you not read a damn BOOK!? Your mom's uterus was bound to up the dosage of glitter and show tunes after that whole quidditch team busted out.

"I play quidditch!"

Fag.

"YOU'RE A FUCKING TORNADO!"

I'm alive enough to know you were never special.

Ron's knees buckled. All thoughts of the sword now cowered away like beaten hounds. Images of his brothers and sister, their moments of glory, ran through his mind.

A treasure hunter, an assistant to the Minister of Magic, two self-employed entrepreneurs… what am I forgetting… oh yes, a FUCKING DRAGON TAMER! The twister rolled a bit; if it had hair to toss, Ron was sure it would have.

"I—I was a school prefect! I played Keeper for our house quid—"

And what about your sister? the twister carried on. *You know, the one Harry bumped uglies with every chance he got?*

Ron tried to punch the smoke, but it burned his hand horribly. He tried kicking it and it threw him back again onto the unforgiving frost.

"Don't listen to it Ron!" Harry screamed from behind the cyclone. So helpful, really. "I don't know what you're hearing, but I figure you're not just yelling about playing Keeper without hearing some sort of… er, voice… that may or may not be challenging your manhood at the moment."

That's where the sting hurts the most, isn't it Ron? You tried so hard to be a man for that Lavender girl, didn't you? Thought if only you could get her in the sack and 'accidentally' show everyone her left-behind panties, you'd be just like Harry: a hero; a curious boy playing under the sheets with his best mate, but straight through and through.

"Don't be stupid!" Ron shouted. He wasn't sure if it was directed at the twister, at Harry, or at himself.

So many girls fell at his feet. Cho, Romilda, Ginny, and of course Hermione's had her little gash out for Harry's wand ever since his balls dropped.

Ron's stomach knotted.

You know he's had them all, don't you? You know, deep down, you were nothing special.

A sting pricked the tip of Ron's nose. The corners of his eyes singed.

"It was special," he murmured.

The twister seemed to lean back. *Honey, two fifteen year olds giving each other hand jobs in the quidditch locker room is not what we call special.*

"It was special to me!" Ron raged, desperate. It was the match that Ron had won; the one Harry didn't even play. The fame was his alone, and Harry seemed so happy for him, so happy that his best friend brought a victory home for the team. In the locker room, Harry's playful shoves had softened, his grip had firmed. His lips had been so... well... so experienced... Ron's mind had reeled all evening after that kiss. How many sleepless nights did he spend scheming about stealing some of Harry's hair to make a potion, magically transform hi s body to look like Harry's, and rub one out with the his best friend's equipment?

The fantasy of course died with Dumbledore. When he was killed, it was Ron whom Harry ran to, Ron's arms in which Harry cried, Ron's bed in which they made love. Harry was all sinew and warm, pale flesh. Ron had been clumsy and nervous. He couldn't believe it was really happening, would spasm uncontrollably and then cringe in humiliation. Harry seemed exhausted from grief, but still an expert somehow.

He'd had practice with all those girls. It was as if the locket had read Ron's mind.

Harry lumbered around the cyclone to get to Ron but the black smoke pushed him into a tree trunk. A loud thud echoed from the impact.

Here's the deal, sweet stuff: you were the second-to-last child, with the baby of the family being the girl your mother hoped you to be. She already had big strapping sons to brag of. And when it became apparent you were nothing to write home about, she took a stray under her wing.

Ron shook his head. "He's my friend."

He's. Your. Replacement. Don't you see? Your mother always cared more about his safety, his wellbeing, always pushing meals on him and trying to protect him from anything she could. And you? She sent you frilly hand-me-down robes for your school dance. A real charmer, you were.

He tasted bile in his throat now. He felt in his gut that everything the locket tornado soul monster was saying was true.

"Don't listen to it, whatever it's saying! Just destroy it!" Harry wheezed from the snow, rubbing his head. "Ron, I need your help with this! You can do it!"

Then he'll take all the credit. No one will remember you were here when the story is retold, the voice cooed. *He'll just keep going until he's the last hero standing. Even if you kick the bucket on the way.*

Something sparked in Ron. Though his gut secretly agreed with everything else the locket said, this part was wrong.

"He cares for me!"

You're an embarrassment to him.

"He needs me!"

Tool!

"HE LOVES ME!"

"YOU'RE PATHETIC!" The cyclone roared, this time out loud. "UGLY, SKINNY, STUPID TEENAGER WITH ACNE AND AN EMPTY WALLET!" The voice was no longer high and cold, nor sassy. It was his own, Ron's, but trenchant somehow, coming from the locket. "NOBODY WANTS YOU! HOW COULD HE LOVE YOU WHEN YOU'RE NOTHING WITHOUT HIM? NO MAN FALLS IN LOVE WITH HIS OWN SHADOW!"

Ron fell to the ground. It was over. He couldn't do anything but bury his head in his hands. He was defeated. Everything was out on the table, his darkest secrets, his honest feelings, bellowed out loud in the forest for Harry to witness like an indecent act that would haunt Ron forever.

The twister's revolutions slowed down, became stationary, a black cloud now blocking out the trees and looming over Ron. He knew it was about to consume him. It was too late. He felt it closing in on his shoulders.

But the grip was unexpectedly tender, and coming from behind him. He turned and saw that it was Harry's hand on his shoulder. His eyes watered behind his glasses, the sword in his free hand. He was holding it out to Ron.

"Ron, I don't… I don't know how to say…" he started. The shadow of the cloud passed over both of them now. It was only a matter of time.

Ron waited.

Harry drew a deep breath. "It was special to me too." He placed the sword in Ron's hand. "I was the one who always had to be in this mess. But you chose it. You stuck with me and risked your life because you… you cared for me so much, and… I know I took it for granted. Your family. You."

Ron could feel the smoke wisp around his hair now. It felt like tragedy incarnate, as if he had forgotten how to hope.
"I kissed Ginny because I was afraid. Cho too. All of it. Ron, I hope you get what I'm trying to say."

The smoke felt like sickly breath on his ears now. Ron shook his head desperately.

Harry gave a mirthless laugh. "Between your thick head and my caught tongue, it's a wonder we can talk at all." He wrapped his hand around Ron's fingers, around the sword. "What I'm trying to say is… you're braver than I could ever be. You aren't hiding your love for me. But I was hiding from you. From everyone." His bright green eyes pierced into Ron's. "You're the special one."

Just as the smoke crept down Ron's spine, he felt Harry's lips against his. It wasn't quite romantic, he supposed, what with a billowing cloud of Dark locket skank trying to kill them both and a rather teary kiss. It would also be the last time they ever had a sword between them while making out. But it snapped Ron into consciousness. Somehow he had never thought it before, but now it was plainly clear as if he could see himself through Harry's eyes: he was the helper. He was the loyalist. He was honest and strong and had real feelings. Red-headed, tall, lanky, pale, and gay as a maypole, he was a whole person, even without The Chosen One.
It was over in a flash of red. Harry gasped, then there was a low hissing sound. The locket shrieked when Ron destroyed it with one strike from the sword.

GIIIIINGEEEEER BIIIITCH!

It took a while for Ron to catch his breath. He kept the sword in one hand. With the other, he made his way to pick up the twisted metal debris in the snow. But he found his hand already full when Harry took hold of it.

It took a significant amount of willpower not to throw Harry onto the ground and make a frenzied, two-person snow angel.

"This is yours," Harry whispered, picking up the destroyed locket and handing it to Ron. It was morning now.

They began walking away from the pond, up the snowy slope through the thick trees toward Harry and Hermione's camp. Ron had never held a man's hand before.

"Let me tell Hermione about the locket. You always get the glory," he said as they plodded through the snow.

"Sure," Harry replied. "But I get to tell her about us."

Ryan Crawford

is an Oregonian transplant living in Seattle, Washington, working at a tobacco cessation company. His poetry and short stories have been published in *Fragments, Censor This!, Mastadon Dentist, Cerebral Catalyst*, and *Gay City Volume 3: Re-Pulped*. He maintains a healthy relationship with soul music.

Love Potion Number Nine

Steve Dunham

Sitting in my adoptive city of Chicago's huge Holy Name Cathedral one warm Sunday, waiting for an organ recital to begin, I noticed how the sun, streaming through the Matisse-like windows, illumined the tawny marble walls and forest of slender columns, like sheaves of rosy phallic asparagus – and my gaze particularly fastened upon the rows of cherrywood confessionals clustered on either side of the transept.

Then I noticed, among the sparse audience on this summery afternoon, a handful

of good-looking young guys in pairs, threes, or singly – some with backpacks, some just off skateboards – dressed not to hear Bach but to enjoy a brief recess in the Cathedral's air-conditioning. Their sweaty tank tops and clingy shorts showed off lithe, tan bodies; smooth legs, slightly hairy, glowing in the borrowed light.

The combined images of these confessionals and sexy youths brought back delectable recollections from a long time ago, when my hometown teenage clique back in Ohio attended a private Catholic prep school for boys, affiliated with the parish of Gesu Church.

While the splendors of Holy Name are ever fresh in my mind, I have only a hazy picture of old Gesu. It stood along one of our city's posher boulevards, but was itself a diminutive rather than imposing edifice. Its rust-colored terra cotta facade offered a screen of Romanesque arches reminiscent of background architecture in Giotto tryplichs. Inside I can only recall gloom, malevolent green stained glass – and an infamous confessional booth.

Our favorite priest was Father Ryan, a 30ish buzz-cut guy – handsome in what today we would call a Kevin Bacon way. He ruled the history classroom, athletic field, and locker room by day and Gesu Church's confessionals day and night. Because of his academic responsibilities, Father Ryan's church duties were limited to pretty much what he wished to do there. The Monsignor heading our school officiated at most masses, and other faceless clerics assisted with sacraments and confessions, but the good Father was in charge of every detail of decorum and regimen, including who ought to confess in which booth.

Gesu's confessionals were free-standing cabinets which a parishioner entered

in front and the priest through his own little door in back , avoiding face-to-face contacts.

The dozen booths stood along either side of the nave, each marked with a tarnished brass numeral. On the right side were booths seven through twelve, but the doors to numbers eight and ten were perennially locked because Father Ryan's special cubicle was Number Nine. He didn't want anybody occupying Eight or Ten to hear certain activities inside Nine.

In the vestibule hung a carved wooden cupboard, something like an old-fashioned hotel message case, with exactly twelve square pigeonholes, one for each confessional station. Nesting in each hole was an ivory sphere about the size of a bocci ball, incised with a numeral one through twelve. At designated times of day or evening, communicants wishing to confess approached the cabinet, selected a ball, and walked directly to the booth they had selected. Shortly, whichever priest on duty surveyed the cabinet and entered the designated boxes from behind to console the penitent. If a person arrived to find all the white balls gone, he would sit on the hard vestibule bench and wait until someone exited the sanctuary and handed over his ball. Woe be unto anyone who, in ecstasy or despair, forgot to turn in their ball!

It was tacitly understood among the other clergy that Father Ryan's special booth was Number Nine, reserved exclusively for hearing the confessions of us troubled, handsome schoolboys. Coincidentally, about the time the good Father was assigned to Gesu Parish, a popular song high on the national teenage music charts, "Love Potion Number Nine," became a huge inside joke among us– referring to all the "love potion" we guys expended inside "Number Nine" thanks to Father Ryan's ministrations.

If the right boy came in, he might be in the box for as long as twenty minutes. My own visits to Number Nine were frequent, fun, and neither excited me excessively nor scarred me for life, as many claim such experiences did – years later attributing their silence to fears of the priest and of guilty pleasures . All the less religious Catholic boys, whether straight or gay, joke about randy priests and either brush them off without recriminations or actually cooperate if rewards are offered.

Alone of all the confessionals, because of its special function, Number Nine had no kneeler but it did have a unique feature – hardly noticeable – that the others lacked. Exactly waist-high from where a fellow stood was a little double door which opened inward, about twelve inches square, installed at Father Ryan's direction and exactly blending in with the dark old wood of the cubicle.

My best buddy Teddy's experiences in Number Nine were exactly like mine and the others in our clique, except for how he dealt with it – vengefully!

Teddy would enter and, after the preliminary mumbled niceties, allowed Father Ryan
to open the little doors and gently caress the front of his pants, unzip them, do sensuous things, and send Teddy away ecstatic.

Teddy's confessions accelerated to several a day, and he confided to me that he was in love with Father Ryan – who paid almost no attention to him outside of the cubicle. One afternoon, hoping to spark the priest's ardor, Teddy bared his backside and pressed it against the opening. His confessor took the bait, but when he was finished commanded Teddy never to darken Number Nine again.

Crushed, Teddy determined that very night to assert his passion regarding another infatuation he was harboring.

The object of his desire was Brad, a new junior classmate who had joined us mid-term after being kicked out of an Eastern school. He was easily the most beautiful, manly specimen in our midst, already a football star and dater of sassy girls from our sister academy, Saint Ursula. Somewhat of a loner, he gamely tolerated Teddy's fawning, up to a point.

The evening of Father Ryan's rejection, Teddy impetuously invited Brad for a sleep over, their first and last.

After Brad had dozed off, Teddy attempted something we old-time collegians call "the Princeton Rub." Teddy hugged Brad ferociously and shot off between his befuddled bedmate's silky thighs, all the while pretending to be asleep. Brad – who was not asleep – took his pillow and the bedspread and retreated to the bare floor, as far from Teddy as he could get.

Teddy felt miserable the rest of the night, not knowing what Brad would say in the morning. He said nothing, merely left the house at daylight.

The thing which had emboldened Teddy in the first place was that, prior to nodding off, Brad had tearfully confided to him a great dilemma – Monica Malone, a hoody cheerleader from the wrong side of the tracks, had accused him of getting her pregnant and had dire consequences in mind. These were the days when high school motherhood was not shrugged off, a time when rich girls were "sent away" and poor girls demanded marriage. Monica had threatened to tell her father and brothers – who were the closest to what passed in our town for gangsters. Teddy could offer no advice, and his sexual advances had not only surprised Brad but disgusted him.

Angry at rebuffs by both Father Ryan and his new friend, Teddy cornered Brad a few days later, apologized, and suggested that he seek a special consultation about Monica with the very astute Father Ryan, even offering Brad the physical company of himself and me to introduce him to the procedure.

Amazingly, Brad agreed. He climbed the church steps with us, selected ball Number Nine, and upon his entering Father Ryan's confessional Teddy and I knelt in the nearest pew with a clear sight line, our eyes glued to the cubicle door and our ears cocked to hear the telltale click of a belt buckle plus the rustle of falling boxers.

"YEE-AAGGHH!" was what we heard, an enraged Father Ryan.

Brad burst through the door, his open pants soaking wet. He had peed profusely in his confessor's face!

Glaring at us, the hunky football star hurled his ivory ball at a porcelain icon of the Christ Child, knocking off its head, and raced down the aisle and out. Later Brad, his father, and his uncle, a powerful attorney, charged into the Monsignor's office without an appointment.

That very evening Father Ryan vanished.

Not long afterward, his special confessional was locked up tight and its flanking neighbors unlocked, the keys and cueballs discovered in one of Father Ryan's desk drawers. For a time, it was the end of "Love Potion Number Nine."

But not forever! My old pal Teddy tells me that, although most of our old crowd have moved far and wide – including Brad and Monica, now grandparents -- Gesu Church is ever growing, if gloomy. Confessional Number Nine has been re-opened, a proper kneeler installed, but its little wooden doors left intact. Occasionally along comes a priest who appreciates and perpetuates their purpose, with utmost discretion.

Steve Dunham

Steve's stories have appeared in *Genre Magazine* (garnering the 2001 Maggie Award for Best Fiction by the Western Publications Association). Others have been featured in gay fiction anthologies, twice by Alyson and three times by The Haworth Press– most recently in Michael Luongo's noted and controversial *Gay Travels in the Muslim World*. Steve's most reviewed work is a pair of edgy novellas, *Tales of Teddy* and *Afternoon in the Balcony* (www.AuthorHouse.com). He lives with his longtime partner in Savannah and Chicago.

The End of an Era

Gregory L. Norris

The end came as the prisoners of the island prepared for the Winter Candlemass carnival. A lone whirlybird touched down on Sugar Beach, at the same level spot where other delegations had landed in previous years. Alone, the Captain strolled out to meet the representative from the Anarchic States government, which had banished the 311 men and women to the desolate lesser atoll, once known as Lost Hope. It had been renamed Samer Island following the forced relocation.

The Anarchic officer identified himself as Commandant Mallette. He was younger than his predecessor, Commandant Bordine. The Captain didn't offer his hand. Mallette likely wouldn't have accepted the gesture anyway. Birchard's respect multiplied for the Captain, who had once stood before a tribunal of his superiors, dressed in his crisp Anarchic military uniform with its brass buttons, and had proudly declared himself a Samer.

Birchard Trent, Lady Judith Rathburn, and Joseph Rhodes watched the two men advance toward the iron gate surrounding the village. Anarchic sharpshooters tracked them with their rifles from the beach. Others in the community trusted with stringing strands of golden-white lights among the calliope horses and carnival rides halted their work. Some halted their play. A unicycle twice Joseph's height – and Joseph was a tall man at six-foot-three – skidded to an awkward stop. Its driver, attired in top hat, amethyst goggles, and a fetching pea coat with a purple fringe of epaulets, gracefully dismounted and assumed a defensive pose with arms crossed.

"At ease," the Captain said as he and Mallette passed by.

The man stepped back. The Captain and Commandant Mallette strolled through the mote of towering black iron fence and into the village at the island's center.

"Sycophant," Lady Judith hissed under her breath.

"Agreed," said Joseph, a man of few words.

"Shhh," Birchard admonished. "I'm trying to listen."

The small device secreted in his left ear, aimed at the Anarchic commandant and the unofficial leader of their society, picked up the gist of a seemingly normal conversation.

"Impressive, Captain Corvallis," said Mallette. "I'd read the report and heard the stories, but I never imagined you'd accomplished so much here in so short a time on Lost Hope."

"Samer Island," the Captain corrected.

Mallette flashed a slippery grin, revealing a length of perfect white teeth that made the gesture seem more snarl than smile. "I stand corrected."

The Anarchic States commandant gazed across the brick downtown, at the carnival rides being readied, and up at the clock tower at the center of the town square, quietly tolling the passage of time. Billows of steam swept around the village, whistling out of storm drain covers set at intervals in the cobblestones and iron chimneys.

"It's a magnificent tribute to your innovation," Mallette continued.

"When living on an island and surrounded by water, wise folk use the resource most readily available to them," the Captain said. "There are many wise minds here."

"No doubt," Mallette said. "Thank you, Captain, for what has been a very enlightening visit."

"Likewise."

He walked Mallette back to Sugar Beach and the whirlybird. Calmly, the Captain waited for them to depart. The whirlybird made a pass over the village, banked to starboard, and then headed out over the gray winter ocean. Once the flying machine was gone from sight, the Captain turned and marched back through the iron gate, and one didn't need an ear piece or a telescopic monocle to understand that their situation had never been graver.

116

"As we suspected," the Captain said grimly to the waiting crowd. "They're close by. That flying machine is only capable of short-range travel. It would not surprise me to discover they've committed an entire battle group to their effort."

As it turned out, their oppressors had sent two.

Birchard studied Joseph as the other man leaned over and gazed into the powerful brass telescope. Joseph James Rhodes was, in Birchard's estimation, the handsomest man on the island. On this island Earth, he thought, cracking a weak smile. On the secret observation deck hidden behind the giant clock face, Birchard caught a hint of Joseph's clean, masculine scent among the gear oil and the warm billows of salty steam. Joseph's vintage leather coat rode up enough to show a teaspoon of lower back and the elastic waistband of his underwear. Old combat boots and uniform pants completed the picture.

"There they are, like the Captain said they would be."

Joseph righted. Despite his fear that the Anarchic States military was returned to finish what they'd started five years earlier when the last convicted Samers were relocated to Lost Hope following the Stonewall Massacres, Birchard's heart galloped for another reason. Joseph's dark cowlicks and emerald gemstone eyes gave him the energy to look. Birchard aimed his right eye into the telescope's viewer. The battle group lolled at the limit of the horizon, two carriers and numerous escort ships.

"Oh my Goddess. How many attack planes?" he asked.

"A lot."

Before he had been forced to confess, Joseph, like the Captain, had served in the Anarchic States military. A former aircraft mechanic, he would know the exact numbers.

Birchard closed his eyes and straightened. When he dared to look again, Joseph was there, and Birchard wanted to believe everything would be all right. Only it wasn't, and the borrowed time they'd all been living on since Stonewall, when politicians and a dictatorship turned prejudice into policy, would soon expire.

"We don't have long," Birchard said.

Joseph said nothing, only fixed him with a wounded look and nodded.

Birchard wanted reassurance, and to reassure. I love you, Joseph, he tried to say, but like the ex-military man of few words, Birchard's tongue stilled. A cold winter wind cycloned around the clock tower, and the forces dispatched to cleanse the island of all life moved closer.

A lilting, melancholy melody drifted out of Lady Judith's cottage, a one-story structure at the edge of the village within clear view of the sheltered lagoon between Sugar Beach and the rocky headlands.

Birchard approached the front door, which was decorated in a mosaic of seashells and bright red holly berries, a sharp contrast to the moody music issuing from inside the cottage. He hesitated from knocking but eventually did. Lady Judith answered the door dressed in a frayed kimono. Eyeliner made from wood ashes had dripped down her face on a cascade of dark tears.

"Birchard," she said, her voice deeper than usual.

Birchard forced a smile. "If this is a bad time…"

Lady Judith answered with a humorless giggle. "Actually, it's a great time. I'm trying to decide on what to keep and what to toss. Come on in."

Birchard entered the house. The once-elegant artwork Judith had been renown for in her other life, pre-island, which had been smuggled over along with her wardrobe and her music, lay in tatters at the center of the plank floor. So, too, were most of Lady Judith's elegant stage clothes.

"Why?" he asked.

She parroted Birchard's question in response.

"Lady Judith?"

"They're coming back here to slay everyone on their little island ghetto. Perhaps they want your technology, to study what we've accomplished here – the smelting plant, the mechanics of steam. They'll pick through the rubble for anything of value. Original Judith Rathburn paintings still command a high price in the art world, out there." Her blackened eyes took on a distant look before also darkening on the insides. "I'd destroy my art rather than allow it to pass into their bloodied clutches."

"Judith," Birchard started, reaching for her shoulder.

Judith pulled away. Her kimono slipped, and the ugly scar she had been branded with during the days leading up to the relocation became visible. Birchard had seen the burn mark once, very briefly, some seasons back on Sugar Beach. Every day since, the scar had remained out of sight, hidden behind exquisite couture, the last gasp of modesty of a famous creature loved and worshipped by many men, despised by others. That she left the kimono as it was without moving to cover the scar stunned Birchard almost as much as the nightmare brewing off the island's shore.

"I don't care about art, not today," Judith said. "Can you imagine what it was like that day when they stormed into my home, when they set my studio on fire?"

Birchard started to speak but the question, he soon realized, had been posed to the walls, knowing they wouldn't answer.

"They should have killed me then, as they killed Phillipe when he tried to put out the flames. No, instead they dropped me here, an artist with no canvases, no paints nor brushes; a cross-dresser without her Phillipe."

"The Captain has called a meeting in the town square to discuss the carnival."

"The carnival," Lady Judith huffed.

In that moment, her uncommon beauty vanished, and the five years of life on Samer Island heaped onto what she had already suffered caught up, showing clearly in her features, upon her shoulders.

"We have to prepare," Birchard said. "All of us, you included."

"I believe that I was." Judith spread her arms, indicating the carnage. "Even if we are to make a run to safety, even then, I know space will be tight, and there are but a few things I wish to bring with me."

Now, Judith seemed willing to invite conversation.

"What things, Lady Judith?" Birchard asked.

Judith plodded into the bedroom. She returned with a swatch of bright purple satin. "Only these. Bold admirers of mine went back, after the Anarchic soldiers left and the fire burned down."

She rolled the cloth between her hands. An oaken, hollow noise rippled through the room and clawed at Birchard's ears.

"Phillipe," said Lady Judith. "I won't leave his bones behind in this cursed place."

"It is brilliant," said Joseph.

The haunted atmosphere that had followed Birchard since his visit to Lady Judith's cottage on the beach lifted some. He focused on the other man's voice. Joseph, handsome Joseph, stood with his arms folded and was following the test run of the amusement rides the way a cat might a bird or a traveling beam of light, partially hypnotized by raw excitement.

Joseph blinked himself out of the trance and turned away from the amusement park jets making passes around a course on heavy cables and the towering rockets rocketing on circular tracks. Their eyes met and, for the thousandth time, Birchard felt a lesser version of the same spark that had given life to the universe explode within his heart.

"You're brilliant," Joseph said.

Birchard stepped closer. The tears he'd barely kept in check at Judith's and after, during this final test of the carnival rides, drove past his barriers. The tears fell suddenly, in torrents. The hard look on Joseph's face softened, as much as a man like Joseph was capable. He growled Birchard's name and extended both hands.

Birchard met him halfway. "I love you," he whispered into the shoulder of Joseph's coat.

"Yeah, me, too," Joseph said.

Birchard gazed up. The barest of smiles cracked Joseph's game face, his war mask.

"Yeah," Joseph repeated, nodding. The warmth and strength of his embrace drove out most of the day's chill. The love in Joseph's twin emerald eyes vanquished the rest. Then Joseph leaned forward, and they kissed.

Somewhere in the distance, a fighter jet screamed across the winter sky.

The Captain took to the podium. His eyes scanned the crowd. With his heart attempting to throw itself up his throat, Birchard had done the same, taking count of heads, goggles, and hats. The Captain made 311. The entire community was present.

The brass bullhorn fixed into the podium broadcast a sharp whine ahead of the Captain's voice.

"People of Samer Island, my fellow, proud Samers," he began. "Behind us lies the humiliation, the persecution, and the atrocities forced upon us all by the Anarchic States following the events at Stonewall. Knowing this day would eventually come, we have lived our lives the best we could, under far from ideal circumstances. I doubt I alone won't miss the endless meals of salted fish and grilled seaweed."

Enough good-natured laughs and a few amens sounded from the crowd, breaking apart the ominous pall that hung over the carnival grounds.

"We knew our oppressors would return, and also that when they did, it would be to deliver one final stroke of pain and bloodshed. But we will show them that we are not sheep, we are not easy victims. We are the best minds, the most talented artists, and the noblest of lion-hearted warriors this world has ever known. And we will prevail."

"How?" someone asked. To Birchard's ear, the voice sounded like Lady Judith's.

"Because we must," the Captain said.

The fingers of Birchard's left hand wandered and found warmth in another, stronger set. Joseph's intertwined with his.

"We must."

Applause sounded, sparse at first. Others joined in, and the level surged to cacophonous, echoing across Sugar Beach and out across the water, in the direction of the approaching storm. It was the first time since preparations for the winter carnival began that Birchard felt a true measure of hope. His grip on Joseph's hand tightened.

"The hours are short," the Captain continued after the applause powered down. "We'll need everyone's help on final preparations for the carnival, so without further delay, let's make this one for the history books that will be written in favor of a handful of Samers who prevailed against the merciless Anarchic States and their war machine."

Birchard Trent, who had excelled in numerous fields of technology and science at an early age before the relocation, marched with Joseph into the heart of the clock tower. They walked among the gigantic gears and springs, to the core where the energy controls feeding power across the island into homes, businesses and, most importantly, the carnival were housed.

The Captain stood at the power board, illuminated by the ghostly golden-blue light arcing between the two pylons secretly located in the belfry. The clock tolled five on an overcast December Saturday, the last day that Samers would spend on Lost Hope, a ferrous atoll whose oxidized landscape lay rusty with the color of spilled blood.

A hand-drawn map of Samer Island stood on an easel. Representations of the naval ships they had spotted through the telescope were marked and plotted. The Anarchic States had surrounded them effectively.

Birchard tore his eyes away from the rudimentary sea vessels and instead focused on the concentric circles he, himself, had only recently added to the map in black from one of Lady Judith's eyeliner pencils. The largest circle traveled almost to the edges of the map, well past the Anarchic naval fleet. The others tightened around the island. The bull's eye was within the iron mote surrounding the village, the clock tower at its dead center.

"I thought it fitting that you should throw the switch," the Captain said.

Birchard reached a trembling hand toward the control.

"Time?" asked Joseph.

Birchard glanced at the countdown clock. "T-minus twenty seconds."

The clock ticked down, the last ten almost the longest of his life, overshadowed only by the ugly moment when he was dragged across campus blindfolded, his name on the seditions list. Then, Birchard was sure that he was going to be shot like so many others. Those seconds had dragged past slower.

The last of the twenty ran out. Birchard turned the brass switch. The energy crackling between the pylons altered. One side dimmed, while the other glowed twice as brightly. Across the island, lights went out inside bungalows, cottages, and establishments. For an instant, only the clock tower defied the snow-swept darkness.

And then an effulgence of golden light rose up from the carnival grounds and into the overcast sky, a bright beacon proclaiming that the Winter Candlemass carnival had begun, and a clear target to the enemy jet fighters that were, even then, launching en masse for the slaughter.

A million golden lights, their bulbs blown from grains of sand meticulously harvested from Sugar Beach, formed constellations around the rocket rides and the jet planes. Calliope horses that Lady Judith had designed and carved from driftwood with the help of numerous other hands galloped around the track to an organ's thrumming beat. Steam billowed. Snow fell. Music and lights defied the approaching storm.

Concession vendors handed out treats to each carnival goer: honey cakes with dried berries wrapped in pale paper painstakingly crafted from bark, crisp water bottled in bottles that had washed ashore over the years or that were smuggled in by the admirers who braved Anarchic blockades of the island, deep-fried fish, golden brown and nourishing.

Each person took their treats and entered the lines, some to the rocket rides, the rest to the jets. The calliope horses raced in an endless circle without riders.

The organ music pumped, striking Birchard's ear like a dirge; a funeral song for the prisoners of Samer Island.

Four dozen warplanes launched from the decks of the monstrous naval platforms that had hemmed in the island, effectively cutting off the seventy-odd acres of rock that had, in five years time, given rise to a technologically-advanced community. The war planes assumed a staggered-wing formation and were ordered to open fire, to level everything and destroy everyone, every last aberrant Samer.

Lights appeared on the horizon, cold white lights and lights the color of blood. The lights grew brighter as the swarm moved closer.

"Here they come," the Captain bellowed. "Move quickly people. Quickly and orderly."

Whimpers and one shrill scream rose in counterpoint against the calliope's dirge. Birchard stood beside Joseph at the back of the line to the rocket ride, waiting for the last of the designated passengers to board. The lights in the sky grew brighter. Joseph's face, Birchard noted, had hardened once more, but gone was his fear. Now, there was only anger and determination in his expression.

Birchard glanced over to the ten jets on the jet ride. The Captain was helping the last of those designated passengers onboard – Lady Judith, who cradled the swaddle of purple satin in her hands. Despite the magnitude of the moment, he was patient and gentlemanly with her, and, even at the distance, Birchard saw very clearly the spark of something bigger between them that hadn't been able to ignite before, shining now as vibrantly as the million lights of their winter carnival.

The Captain and Lady Judith boarded their jet. Birchard and Joseph hurried up the ramp to their rocket. Inside, the passengers had strapped in and cradled their most beloved possessions. A black and white cat named Ozzie poked her head out of the neck of an older gentleman's heavy trench coat.

"We're going to be okay," Birchard said to Ozzie's protector, who'd once been a poet in that lost life before Samer Island.

He and Birchard raced up the aisle and into the cockpit. Joseph quickly assumed the pilot's controls. Birchard moved before the cranks and the levers, the buttons and bright diodes of the control board linked to the clock tower.

"Do it," Joseph urged. "Punch it, before they get any closer!"

Birchard spun corkscrewing cranks, stepped on pedals, and flipped toggles, a mad sequence of movements, but the proper one. "I'm doing it," he said, keying in the final directive.

The unit puffed steam. Birchard waited for the big green glass button at the center of the console to light. Green, though nowhere near the intense color of Joseph's eyes. It did. He punched it.

Nothing happened. The lights outside swarmed closer.

Eyes wide and unblinking, Birchard muttered an expletive and ran the sequence again, only to suffer the same results.

"Birch," Joseph grumbled, the panic in his voice rising, obvious. "The air over our heads is about to fill up with an awful lot of Anarchic warplanes."

Birchard turned. "There's something wrong between here and the clock tower. I'll need to activate the defense manually."

He started back toward the hatch. Joseph caught his arm as he tried to pass.

"You can't. I won't leave you behind."

Birchard spun around, seized Joseph's handsome face between his hands, and kissed him. "You have to," he said when their lips parted. "For them."

With a tip of his chin, Birchard indicated the thirty other souls strapped into their seats. He pulled free of Joseph. One final glance, and he was gone.

A sound like thunder crackled through the snowy sky, the unmistakable battle cry of angry birds streaking in formation to attack. The funeral music from the calliope horses had evaporated; Birchard knew by the image of the static merry-go-round that the malfunction originated there, below the circling gears and treads that had been set up to disguise the true nature of their operation to the eyes of satellites and drones. The circling power source had stopped its revolutions. Something in the treads, a gear or rough section of iron pipe, had cut the line to the clock tower. It made ironic sense when Birchard stopped to consider the morbid melody, a funeral song. If he didn't activate their great defense manually and soon, no one would make it off Samer Island. All would die here.

He ran through the lights and the wind-stirred curtains of powdery white, not fully realizing that he would likely not survive the coming barrage or that, if he did, he'd be left behind here, alone on the island. He only thought of the others – the Captain, Lady Judith, and especially Joseph – and crossed the distance to the clock tower, whose face he would always remember had stopped at 5:11. It was the end of an era.

Deafening screams tore across the sky. The atmosphere inside the clock tower was no less turbulent. Energy pulsed through the air, making it ripple under the stress of the massive power being pumped through conduits and conveyers. Steam hissed from vents, enough to cloud the way to the defense controls.

Joseph. Suddenly, tears spilled out of Birchard's eyes, adding to his confusion. He'd taken this same course through the gears, toward the pylons, thousands of times. He could find his way asleep, or blind. But thoughts of never seeing Joseph again threatened to paralyze him.

The clock tower trembled. The lone pylon channeling energy into the carnival crackled with a blinding nimbus of golden light, blue around the edges. Sparks showered down from that smaller but no less spectacular version of the sun.

Steeling himself, Birchard wiped his eyes on his sleeve and soldiered forward. For Joseph. For the Samers. The pylon would shake itself apart if he didn't act soon and discharge the prominence. Were that to happen, they wouldn't need to worry about the attack by warplanes – the explosion would take out all of Samer Island. While approaching the control board, Birchard prayed to Brigid, to the Saints, to the Goddess or God or whatever other deity might be up there listening. He invoked Joseph's name. That seemed to do it.

Birchard came out of the fog and found himself standing directly before the manual defense controls. He quickly ran through the proper sequence of toggles and whirls and reached both hands toward the all-important green glass button.

"For you Joseph, my love."

Birchard punched the button. Nothing happened.

And then, something did.

The destructive energy crackling around the pylon stabilized. A golden effulgence of light formed at the apex of the construct, a sun as bright and beautiful as anything ever seen in the sky. The sun danced at the top of the pylon, radiant and lovely, a vision from mythology, a gift from the gods. There one moment and gone the next, the sun turned black, becoming a toy of the devil.

The black sun went nova, fanning out around the pylon like a vast dark ring tossed around a pike. Racing downward, the energy shot into the conduits and channels underground. The clock tower quaked with its passing, the disturbance powerful enough to knock Birchard off his feet. While on the floor, he imagined what would happen in short order, this insane plan they'd initiated so long ago.

He was right.

Warplanes streaked toward the island, readying to strafe the carnival grounds. The naval fleet surged closer to the shore.

The energy slammed into the ground, traveled through conduits, and into the mote of iron gates surrounding the village. The electromagnetic pulse then surged upward, into the sky, catching the planes upon their approach. Targeting systems shorted out. Avionics followed. Warplanes tumbled out of the sky.

The E-M pulse continued outward and slammed into the naval fleet. Lights went dark. Vessels broke formation and fell off course. Some collided.

Birchard picked himself up. "Go," he shouted out loud. "Get out of here, now – escape!"

The E-M pulse had turned the world dark everywhere, except for the carnival.

"It worked," Joseph whispered. "The pulse knocked out their technology, but not ours, not the steam!" He punched in the proper ignition sequence. The rocket trembled. "Hold on, everyone," Joseph called out. "Here we go!"

Jets began moving around the track and gained speed. One at a time, they detached from cables, shooting into a snowy sky no longer filled with enemy fighters. Rockets sped down their tracks, jumping them and assuming formation among the jets. The rocket piloted by Joseph soared up on a golden comet's tail.

Birchard staggered out of the clock tower in time to see the fleet formation rise triumphantly higher, above the fires and wreckage of the downed Anarchic warplanes and the scuttled sea vessels. Golden light far more spectacular than the strings wreathed around the remains of the carnival lit the sky, a tribute to the resourcefulness and determination of the Samers, who had bested their persecutors.

"Go now and live without fear," Birchard said, and though tears streamed from his eyes, a wide and happy smile lit his face.

Only they didn't go, as he implored. A lone light, one of the brightest of the comets, came down from the snow clouds. A rocket landed. The hatch trundled open. Joseph walked out.

"I won't leave you behind, and neither would the others," he said.

Birchard forced his eyes away from Joseph and up into the sky, where the effulgence of lights stood stationary.

"Come on," Joseph said.

Birchard hurried toward the hatch. Joseph pulled him into his arms, and they kissed.

"I love you," Joseph said.

Birchard rested his face in the warm spot between Joseph's neck and check. Then they boarded and the rocket rose back into the sky, where it joined the rest of the fleet high above Lost Hope.

"You didn't follow the plan," Birchard said.

From the pilot's seat, Joseph countered, "Neither did you."

Birchard hid his smile. "So now where do we go? To visit those fun-loving French? Those resolute Russians?"

"I don't think so," Joseph said. "I'm sure the Captain would agree that we stick to our original course and head south, far away from the Anarchic States, where we'll find a safe place to live and rebuild."

The beginning of this new era already seemed uncertain. But the plan had worked, and he was with Joseph, and Birchard somehow knew that all would be okay, wherever they landed.

Gregory L. Norris

dreamed "The End of an Era" pretty much as it is written. Norris is a former screenwriter on two episodes of Paramount's Star Trek: Voyager series and author of the handbook to all-things-Sunnydale, *The Q Guide to Buffy the Vampire Slayer* (Alyson Books). Visit him online at: www.gregorylnorris.blogspot.com.

Masquerade

Ted Cornwell

Dr. DeStuysen, it would later be learned, was not really a doctor; at least not of the kind he had allowed people to presume. He was however, very rich. In the 1970s, there were those who believed he belonged on the Fortune 400 list, and only avoided such distinction by concealing his wealth out of a general fear of publicity and scrutiny. The truth of that is uncertain, though he definitely was, by way of inheritance, wealthy enough to own Prospero House on Fire Island.

Prospero House had been a legendary place of gaiety and revelry for decades, with its eight bedrooms and five baths. The house, facing the beach in the Pines, was among the oldest still standing in that community. While big storms known as Nor'easters had reduced many of its neighbors to kindling over the decades, Prospero House persevered much longer than could have been expected. Even a hurricane in the 1950s failed to fell it, though parts of the house had to be reconstructed.

The bedrooms, on two levels, all opened out onto a two-floor living and dining salon, but this was not like some Courtyard Marriott. The rooms each had windows, flanked by candelabra that were occasionally lit to illuminate the grand inner ballroom and bathe it in flickering oranges and golds. On the beach side of this grand ballroom stood an absurdly large grandfather clock, which was flanked by two huge windows overlooking the ocean. Prospero House had been built by a set designer who painted all the bedrooms with different themes, many inspired by classical times. There was a Venetian room and a Theban room. But there was also a Cowboy Room and a Tarzan room.

This was in 1982, just as gay-related immune deficiency had begun to spread panic throughout New York City. Dr. DeStuysen's wealth was so extensive that he had multiple homes on both coasts. He also had a manse in his native Saint Paul, Minnesota, where he spent some of each summer, hosting parties for a bevy of blue eyed, blond haired college students and twenty-somethings who caught his eye. Several of his prodigies had even traveled with him to his Park Avenue apartment in New York, and one or two had even made a name for themselves as models or actors who won small, sexy parts in soap operas or Broadway plays. His acolytes multiplied and grew sexier as news of these breakthroughs spread in the Midwest.

But GRID forced Dr. DeStuysen into an unfamiliar position. Neither New York nor San Francisco offered refuge from the emerging plague. Nobody knew for sure how it spread. What sort of contact might be safe and what was not? Might it be airborne? Could you get it from drinking out of a glass at a bar? From sitting on a public toilet seat? Nobody yet had useful guidelines to offer, though Dr. DeStuysen had a theory, which comforted many in his assemblages of young men and fellow merrymakers: within six months, not only would scientists find the cause of GRID, but they would also have a vaccine to prevent its spread and remedies to reverse its course. Because of his title, which actually reflected a doctorate in medieval studies from an unaccredited university, people were reassured by his confidence. But he was used to offering reassurance, and he himself remained unsettled by the spreading illness.

Already, one of his protégés in New York had fallen ill, and GRID was suspected. And he'd just learned that a roommate from his own salad days, a time before he'd come into money, was likewise ailing. Spooked by these revelations, he returned early, in May, to his Saint Paul retreat. He gathered up 14 of his choicest, most eager admirers, and persuaded them that the best way to avoid GRID would be to summer at Prospero House in Fire Island, far away from the springboards of disease that cities were at risk of becoming. GRID remained virtually unheard of in the Midwest, and seemed not to have reached the Twin Cities, so he felt confident that his assemblage remained untroubled. Though most of his charges had yet to register much fear about GRID, they were easily persuaded that a summer on Fire Island was in order.

Those few who had jobs quit on short notice. They embarked on their journey, via a chartered jet to New York and two private limousines to the Fire Island ferry station, a week before Memorial Day.

They had little trouble ignoring the smoldering crisis they'd left behind. While it was steamy and humid in the city, the ocean breeze bathed Prospero House in a luxurious calm. The days were long. As May gave way to June, the ocean water warmed enough so that a brisk ocean swim was often enjoyed, and the island's carefree attitude toward clothing allowed Dr. DeStuysen ample opportunity to sit on the ocean side deck of Prospero House and watch his herd of beauties frolicking nakedly in the surf. Once a week the entire household would cross through the Pines to greet a water taxi that brought in a voluminous load of groceries and liquor, which they carried back to Prospero House like a conga line of army ants. People took turns cooking, and everyone looked forward to the night when Dr. DeStuysen himself would make shrimp scampi. There were so many cooks among the company that very fine broiled salmon with leeks, and pork tenderloin smothered in a homemade gravy, also were frequently enjoyed. But the real revelry began well after dinner, as the sun was fading and members of the household emerged from their evening naps. When the old, faded grandfather clock chimed its midnight tones, the sound was often drowned out by the noise of the party.

Dr. DeStuysen himself brought up the idea of a masquerade. Though July had arrived, and with it the height of the summer season on Fire Island, the doctor had taken to wearing long-sleeved shirts, of a heavy linen that did not appear particularly summery. His kaki slacks also looked too autumnal for the season. But nobody inquired why their host had taken to such modesty at the peak of summer. There were plenty of finer bodies to be seen within the house and on the beach. A full moon seemed adequate reason to play dress up, and members of the household scrounged through their skimpy duffel bags looking for clothing that could be fashioned into disguises. This effort yielded little of use, but once they turned their attention to the house's dusty closets, dressers and armoires they found a treasure trove of miscellany adequate to create just about any costume one could envision from the detritus of past guests and residents.

One of Dr. DeStuysen's apostles, a quiet farm boy known as Billie who seemed to virtually disappear most nights amid the cacophony of the louder extroverts, spent much of his time scrounging through boxes beneath a sink in Dr. DeStuysen's master bath looking for supplies for his costume. He also snuck some condiments from the kitchen back to the Velvet Room, which he had to himself now that his roommate had shacked up with two of the other guests in some sort of menage-à-trois in one of the other rooms.

Dr. DeStuysen himself did not so much dress up as he simply accentuated his usual eccentricity, turning even more autumnal with corduroy pants and a shirt festooned with Edwardian foppery. He did manage to dig up a trove of turquoise jewelry – bracelets, rings, and a necklace – that left him looking like a San Francisco flower child from the 1960s. Lately, he'd stopped gelling and styling his hair, and his frizzy tuft of fading blond locks only heightened the effect, leaving him looking like someone yearning for an earlier, more idyllic era to inhabit. A place where one could be forever young.

Among his cast of actual naked beauties, each was transformed into something beautiful but unrecognizable from their usual selves. There was not only a Judy Garland, but also a Liza Minell; a sailor and a Canadian Mountie; a baseball player with a mustache painted on with shoe polish. Peels of laughter so shrill they could be heard by passersby for nearly a mile-long stretch of beach echoed from the house. But the gaiety would soon disintegrate into curses and screams that would silence not only Prospero House, but also every house within half a mile. In fact, it is entirely possible that every dinner table at every house in the Pines was hushed that instant when sweet Billie emerged from the Velvet room, and Dr. DeStuysen took in the full meaning of what he was seeing.

Billie was bandaged from head to foot. Ketchup and steak sauce bloodied his gauze. Something mixed with mayonnaise affected a pussy foam around his mouth. His narrow chin and waif-like physique only exaggerated his sudden descent into a living purgatory. Dr. DeStuysen scanned his physique, at first unsure what to make of it. It wasn't until he saw the purple lesion Billie had stenciled onto his ankle that the doctor realized what apparition he was seeing. He never did find out what dye or ink Billie had used to make that mark.

"Do you think that's funny?" he asked, the bile percolating into his voice slowly at first. "Fucking funny, eh?" he bellowed. Billie said nothing. The grandfather clock's midnight chimes were uninterrupted.

"Disease is a joke to you, I see." The doctor began again, his voice at full throttle. Some guests even had to cover their ears. "Well it's not a damn joke to me!"

The doctor, and some of his company still were under the impression that he was a medical doctor, ripped open his shirt.

"Do you see these? Do you see the skin cancers crawling across my chest? My arms? These purple lesions, my dry mouth, my pissing stools. That's what's going to kill me. I'm getting sicker every day. This masquerade, this summer, will probably be my last. Don't you read the papers? Haven't you seen the stories about how deadly GRID has become?"

Billie finally spoke. "I'm sorry. I wasn't thinking of that. I thought I looked like a zombie."

"A zombie," the doctor boomed, staring at the young man's ankle. (Billie didn't know why the doctor was staring at his feet.) "A zombie with karposi's sarcoma? Get out of my house. Get all your fucking things and get out."

Billie retreated to the Velvet Room, visibly shaken and looking so much more sickly than he had when he first revealed his costume. One of the other acolytes spoke.

"I really think it may have been a mistake. He might not have realized..."

"Not realize what's happening to me? What's happening to us? It's all over the papers. It's getting worse every day. And it's definitely no fucking joke. Not anymore."

"But..."

The doctor cut him off. "I want all of you out of this house. Out tonight. The fucking party is officially over."

They left together, silently, trudging across the thin island to sleep on the dock near the ferry landing. They would take the train into New York City, where some of them would be absorbed into the fabric of a besieged community, while most would limp home to the Twin Cities, wounded in a way they couldn't quite comprehend. They were all between the ages of 21 and 26. None would live to celebrate a thirtieth birthday.

As for their capricious host, he remained alone at Prospero House as summer gave way to fall, enduring his decline without much in the way of medical attention. From what he read – and he alone in the house had been reading all the papers that were delivered along with the groceries and booze – there wasn't much doctors could do anyway. He sat on his deck looking out at the beautiful stretch of beach as the season faded and the gracefully naked young men walking by in the surf or on the sand gradually dwindled to nothing. And still he sat and stared and read the daily papers even as he became very gaunt. He made what arrangements he cared to make via telephone calls to lawyers in New York.

One day a photograph caught his eye in the Sunday edition of the Minneapolis newspaper. Though he had papers mailed in from any city where he had property or investments, the Minneapolis one he skimmed quickly most days. But this story he did not skim.

Sure enough, the photo was of Billie, looking even paler and thinner than Dr. DeStuysen remembered him. In the article, Billie was identified as the leader of an impromptu group trying to draw attention to the GRID epidemic in the Midwest, which had not been spared after all. It was one of the first times the doctor had heard the situation referred to as an epidemic. He was shocked that shy Billie had taken on such a public and vocal role. A state senator was quoted as praising Billie's work, and hearings were being held to attempt to formulate an awareness campaign. The state epidemiologist was allocating quite a bit of funding for research, but acknowledged that what he had couldn't possibly be enough.

In the weeks leading up to the Dr. DeStuysen's death in November, the few visits he received were from lawyers who needed to have papers signed. He hired an island handyman to provide some basic care-taking services, mostly to be sure that his body would not languish undiscovered until the spring.

When he did die, there were obituaries in all the papers he'd subscribed to so loyally over the years. And the obituaries shocked his former acolytes and other friends and acquaintances, who'd presumed his fortune would either be squandered or left to relations as frivolous as he'd been.

Instead, his fortune, which actually totaled more than $100 million dollars, was divided among a number of nascent organizations that had been formed to fight the epidemic that was just starting to be called AIDS. Not only the GMHC in New York but also Billie's group in Minneapolis and organizations in a half dozen other cities across the country. Some money was left to a group in Washington, D.C. that was lobbying for more research into treatment of the condition. There is no way to know if the money hastened any advances in treatment or success in raising awareness of the disease, but it did draw attention to the need that was out there, and the praise heaped upon the doctor for his first and only philanthropic outburst edged some other wealthy donors into joining the fight.

As for Prospero House, it was inherited by a nephew and gradually fell into disrepair so great that it probably would have been raised even if it had not finally been flattened by a big coastal storm a few years after the doctor's death. The site was sold and an even bigger, more audacious home rose in its place. The new house has regained the old Prospero House reputation for hosting the wildest and most coveted parties on Fire Island during the high season of July and August each year.

Ted Cornwell

is a poet, fiction writer and journalist who grew up in Minnesota and has lived in New York City since the mid-1990s. His fiction has appeared in *Gay City Volume 3: Re-Pulped*, as well as in anthologies from Alyson Books, Arsenal Pulp Press, and Cleis Press. He blogs, less frequently than he intends to, at www.poetontheprowl.blogspot.com.

The Shining One

From The Tales of Peleus

Felice Picano

"I'll begin near the end of my story, since that's what everyone is most curious to hear. My first son."

"Achilles. The shining one," I said.

Peleus shrugged.

"What? Achilles wasn't shining?" I had to ask.

"Oh he was shining enough. But he was my son. A father sees every tiny flaw, you understand. And he had his share of them, poor boy. Beginning with his name. You know what his name means, of course, you scholar, you?"

"A-kill-lay," I deconstructed the old Greek, "Without a . . . breast! Why? Didn't he have any nipples?"

"He had lovely nipples. That name was given to him by the chatterboxes in the women's quarters of my court. It signified that he didn't feed from his mother's breast. Thetis was a goddess, remember. She had no milk for him. Only animals like humans made milk and breast-fed their young. Anyway, she was gone by the time he needed milk."

"Gone? Thetis abandoned her son?"

"And me, her husband too. After, I had a breast stitched together of the softest chamois and I fed him myself – warm goat milk. I was his breast feeder. Until he healed. Then some of the girls from the women's quarters said that they were no longer frightened by his appearance and they took pity and they began feeding him too. But by then he was used to the artificial breast."

"Healed? From what?"

"From his mother." Peleus laughed. "Of course being a goddess She always blamed me for what happened."

"Don't stop now!"

"We had been wed almost three years and I loved my beautiful, eternally-seventeen year old goddess-wife as only a teenage boy-king could, so naturally enough I made certain she was pregnant as much as possible.

The children were all born early, four of them, and none of them survived more than a few days. After they were born, I didn't see them until they were shown them to me – dead! They were all red and awful. I thought they looked like most babies after birth. So I paid no heed to it. Just before the fifth was to be born, a seer appeared in our little kingdom of Phthia. I don't recall his name, but he insisted upon gaining entrance to the court.
Naturally he received a guest gift and guest accommodations. For ten days, he said not one word of any special import, and we paid little attention to him, because my goddess-wife gave birth yet again at that time. Having lost four before, all of us were naturally enough, concerned for this fifth child's life.

But he was born at midday with little trouble and he looked fine. Healthy, they all said.

Later that same afternoon, as I came in from hunting with my little entourage, the visiting seer knelt down at one side of my horse, so I had to step on his back in dismounting.

 After I had done so, I was chagrined. "Why must I dishonor you in this way?" I asked.

"For what I am about to tell you, Sire," he whispered fiercely and looked about us. "After that you may do much more than kneel upon me, in your anger."

I sent my men on ahead into the palace and stood alone with him in the courtyard. I was very curious indeed.

When he was sure the others were gone I asked what he wanted of me.

He said, "Take four drops of this draught tonight after you have consorted with your goddess-queen and before your eyes close in exhaustion."

He held out a tiny vial of some unknown metal— tin perhaps, inside a pale blue liquid.

"Is it not true," the seer asked, "That natural fatigue and your Goddess keeps you deeply asleep each night after She has given birth each time?" the seer asked.

"I'm a youth. We frolic. Afterward, I sleep dreamlessly," I admitted.

"But now you must awaken," he said. "These drops will awaken you after you have slept a while."

"Really? Or instead will they keep me from *ever* awakening?"

"As guarantee, I will stay in your guardroom in chains all night. If you come to ill effect from the potion, I'll die."

"But why?"

"Sire, I do not know why, not fully at least. This is the curse of those of us blessed to understand future and past events but never as clearly as we would like. I will explain as best I can. On my way here, I thought to take an afternoon nap from the hot sun and I sought the shade inside what seemed to be some kind of peasant's shack or hut with roughly hewn carved wood columns. Only when I awakened a short while before sunset and could see clearly inside, did I realize that I had slept on the leaf-littered floor of a small old wooden temple. It looked abandoned. It had but one much worn and insect-eaten wooden statue of a woman wrapped in cloths so only her nose and mouth could be seen clearly but those were lovely, supernally sculpted."

"I believe you speak of the little old temple of Rhea," I said. "We honor it once a year. It's said to be the oldest in the land."

"Sire, as I slowly awakened a voice spoke to me, from that statue or I know not where, but a woman's voice, deep as the earth itself. It told me to come to your court, King Peleus. I didn't understand why, until I had left it behind and was walking upon a ridge with a view of the sea, and then I felt something prickling me under my tunic. As I lifted it to look at it in the long sunset-light I saw this vial and on t I read writing that existed ever so briefly. "Awake sleeper!"

"I remembered then that although the temple had been empty when I entered, when I left there was fresh Rosemary plaited into a wreath, interspersed with little mountain gentian flowers. I had smelled it deeply and then placed the wreath upon the head of the statue and said a prayer to all of the Olympians. But you must know, Sire, in the lore of simple herbs, these two flowers mean 'remember long' and 'pain that must be healed'."

"Both the temple and statue you speak of are dedicated to Rhea," I said, "The mother of Zeus."

"Zeus, your own grandfather, Sire," the seer said. "Then the message came direct from your ancestor so surely it was an important one."

I took the vial from him. All during the usual court feast that night I sought to look for the old seer. He ate and drank and gamboled like the others, seemingly relieved now, rather than in any way anxious.

After dinner he came to me and said he was ready for me to put him into chains and into our guardroom, there to be slain if any ill came to me from the vial."

That night I sported with Thetis as usual, unsuspecting, and then as usual I fell to sleep exhausted.

But I had taken the four drops as the seer had instructed when I'd stood to make water, before collapsing onto our bed. So I suddenly awakened again during the night. The torches were all but extinguished in the room. My wife was not in the bed.

I thought she had heard the infant crying and had gone to his side. He was kept in a nearby room, with first wife (in name only) and friend Antigone who loved him as her own and already had experienced two boy children herself.

Antigone lay dead asleep, her hand protectively upon the basket in which the baby had been placed. But my son wasn't there.

Now I was more than curious. I was worried. I kept thinking, the baby is with its mother. It is safe. Yet the worry would not leave me.

I hunted through the sleeping palace for the two. After an hour I was almost maddened by some as yet unformed thought: Had she taken the child? And if so for how long? For what reason? Would she return? Would they return?

The seer's earlier words returned to me. I would mistreat him badly after I knew the truth upon awakening. As yet I knew nothing.

Some of the many courtiers and their companions in the palace stirred a bit as I went by, but all slept soundly, almost as though, as the seer had said to me earlier, they had been willed into dreamless sleep. I wandered into the outer courtyards and into the stables and the various animals' houses, almost frantic now to find them.

Then I saw a light. Only a flicker, but it was from a fire and it came from the shed behind the stables where the blacksmith had his forge for repairing horse-shoes and other metal for our little, single-horse cars and wagons.

I calmed myself as best as possible and trod as silently as I could toward that light.

Her back was toward me and Thetis was so rapt in what she was doing that even her immortal hearing didn't make me out. At first her body blocked my view, then we both moved, she one way a bit and I the other way, and what she was doing in that forge became all too visible.

And what was she doing? She had my baby son lying in a cooking pan upon the forge and it was filled ten inches high with green fire and she was burning him alive. He didn't scream. He didn't fight. He lay limp, in the same stuporous sleep she had willed upon me and all the members of my court.

I suddenly understood why all the other babies had died and why they had been so red when their corpses came to me to be buried. She'd done this to all of them.

She lightly held him by one chubby ankle and she stirred the fire with another, making certain the green flames covered his entire body, much as a chef browns a leg of lamb all over.

So this sight was what the Goddess Rhea had told the seer to have me awaken to witness: possibly the most horrible thing any man could ever see.

I ran at Thetis, and in her being surprised, I was able to thrust her aside.

I grabbed the infant, wrapped him in my robe and ran out. It was as though all in one motion.

The stables held a large water trough and I dumped the baby into it, and did so with him over and over again.

By this time she had caught up to me. But she did nothing but stare at me in my dunking and washing of the sleeping baby, as I dunked him I wept with the greatest rage I have experienced in my life.

140

I wrapped the infant back up in my robe, content at least that all the fire was out. The baby lay as dead, yet I heard it breathing, Its skin was horrible with burns. I could barely look at it.

"Had you thought to ask, I would have told you what I was doing," Thetis finally said, very calmly.

"Killing him like the others. I don't know why."

"No, I was making him immortal. I was making him unkillable. I was bathing him in ambrosia and nectar and even some ichor."

"Like you made unkillable the four others of my seed?"

"It doesn't always work," she admitted. "With this one it seemed to be working."

"He is unkillable now, except where I held him," she said, calmly and just as calmly she explained: "I am entitled to have an immortal son. You are partly divine. I am fully divine. It should be possible."

She reached out for the baby.

"You must kill me first," I said, backing away.

Her absolute coolness and rationality as she spoke drove me into the blackest of fury. Still, I held the child and I held my temper.

"And I?" I finally was able to utter. "Am I not entitled to have one living son of this union that was blessed by dozens of Immortals?"

"Yes. You are," Thetis admitted. "Nor am I allowed to slay you to get what I want..." she added, sadly it seemed.

I was afraid the baby would awaken and begin screaming in pain. We stood there, then, at an impasse.

"Then . . . farewell, husband," she said. She added, musingly, "I told them this marriage would never succeed."

She backed slowly away, into the stable doorway and she spun and was gone. I saw only the glint of the bottoms of her silvery feet as she flitted up into the night.

I rushed to the kitchen and found oils and balms and awakened the seer and I showed him the child.

The seer shook his head sadly. "She has fixed it so he will not remember this. He will love her anyway!"

"You mean she will return?" I asked, fearful.

"In some future year. Not soon. And to him, first," he added. "Now she is angry and will vent her rage on some unsuspecting person or innocent town."

The seer had some healing balms himself and we spread them all over the baby, and then we kept close watch on the infant from that time onward. I even had a kind of leather sling made up to hold the child in front of me at all times, with a fleece inserted for a soft bed, for I feared to let him go from me even at night, when I had guards take turns being awake in the chamber where we slept.

He never cried after that night. His big eyes were curious and alert. His little hands began to grab and hit out soon enough. His skin looked awful for weeks. But when all the crusts and flakes came off, he was as he would always be thereafter, pure of skin, without a mark, mole or blemish, complected golden, not unlike my hair was when I was young. He was, you put it well, a shining one."

"So you were his father – and his mother, both!"

"Yes," Peleus said. "I was, for years, both parents and more. No father of that time had as much stake in his son as I did. He sat on my lap at dinner or on the throne always and he slept next to me in my bed until he was seven years old."

"You were greatly devoted to your son. Unusual"

"Yes unusual. But the Gods gave me great capacity for devotion. . . " Peleus mused. Then he added, "So, I guess you could say that I was doubly betrayed by Achilles."

"Betrayed? How?"

"That's another story, isn't it?"

"Tell me."

"Achilles grew and he was beloved of all the court. Except that is, by the other little boys. There were few enough that he might play with. But after a while he played alone or joined the guards and court soldiers when they did their military exercises. They made him a little sword and spear and helmet and cuirass too. With me he was rough too, but I thought it was mere child's play. Until I asked my steward, Antilochus.

He hemmed, he hawed, he did anything he could not to answer, and then at last he blurted out what I feared.

"The prince cannot stay his hand or his little sword or spear. All the children are wounded by him one way or another and now their mothers keep them indoors whenever they hear the Prince is afoot."

I wondered how to tame the boy, and I feared I could not. As his mother had said to me that last time, his blood was three quarters divine. He himself felt invulnerable and he must have wondered why other children weren't too. His perfect skin seemed unbreakable why should others get cut, bruised and torn?

He had passed his seventh birthday and was he was learning how to fight among my soldiers. By that age, he ignored those guards and court soldiers, his earlier playmates. Every morning after his breakfast of barley gruel and honey, he now walked straight out to the barracks of the Myrmidons, and remained until hunger seized him.

These troops I inherited from the former ruler, my lover, Eurytion. There are many fables about them, and they are not spare of giving mythical backgrounds themselves. One myth says that they were raised into men instantly, out of soldier ants marching upon the ground, and by none other than Our Lord, Zeus, himself. Repayment, or compensation to an ancient king of Phthia named Myrmis. Supposedly the young Divine, Apollo was still testing his powers, and had unwittingly unleashed a plague upon the land, killing all the men.

Whatever their origin, the Myrmidons were of great value to me. Not only because of their well known reputation for fighting together, closely, fiercely, and never leaving one of their wounded behind. That you may imagine kept my kingdom safe from all ideas of invasion, But also because they needed to fight, to hone their skills, and so they begged me to lease them out to other rulers to help fight their wars. The Myrmidons returned to Phthia with scars, with booty, or they returned as shadows, dead in some other land, yet with honor. And I was all the richer by it, and all the more envied."

Achilles now trained with these soldiers, even at his young age. But it was not a proper solution.

Then a solution presented itself to me. Recall, beautiful manly, Aeson, my sometime companion, King of Iolchos who had been so close and helpful a friend to me after the tragic events of the Calydonian Boar Hunt?

He had died. Under circumstances that had always seemed unclear to us. Until that is, his son, Jason came to my court. With him, were several of my other companions of that great hunt, all a few years older now: Castor and Polydeuces, Meleager with the flaming hair, that tantrum-cursed son of Ares. They were on a mission and wished me to join them.

The cause: regaining the throne from Aeson's brother in-law who had seized it and who now held it as "regent," until he said young Jason could prove himself worthy to rule. How could he do so? By obtaining the Golden Fleece of King Aetes in Colchis.

At this time, I had no worries. All was well in Phthia and the land was rich and my courtiers could use a lesson or two in how to be regents themselves, so I joined Jason and my old friends.

It was Jason who suggested that I bring little Achilles to my own savior and to his own mentor, the Centaur Cheiron, in the north of my land, up in the foothills of Mount Pelion.

At first the boy wouldn't go. He wanted to join us on the big-prowed craft he'd heard of abuilding in Thessaly.

But Achilles was curious and he was attracted to the honeyed sentences and the pretty black hair and the smooth body of Jason, an older boy, like himself a Royal Prince, who he could look up to. So he came with us, as the group of us traveled once more up those foothills, and along that Nereid-haunted sea coast where I had encountered, become enraptured by, and then netted my goddess-wife. To keep, I had thought. But that was not to be.

The boy Achilles ate up all this lore as he heard it, the hunt, the heroes — and one heroine, Atlanta — as well as his own past, as it were, and he enjoyed himself on this "bivouac" as he called it. Everything with him was martial.

His first meeting with Cheiron was typical.

Seeing for the first time his new teacher's four strong legs, the small boy Achilles challenged the Centaur to a race! And he gave him a good run for it. The last I saw of them that visit, Cheiron had doubled back, swooped up the boy into his arms and he was tossing Achilles into the air ahead of himself and then racing forward to catch him, and then throwing him again further, and racing to catch him. All to Achilles' great and loud delight, as they headed away from us, ever deeper onto the Olympian massif.

Our voyage on the Argo lasted two years, and for some of us it was rewarding and for others tragic. Heracles lost his *ephebe*, Hylas, his one true love. And we only later came to understand from an oracle that we consulted how Hylas was stolen from Heracles at the behest of his enemy, Ox-eyed Hera. As the boy gathered water at some nameless stream in Cius, tributary into the Sea of Marmara, he was pulled down into the water so that he might become a river-goddess' toy.

I returned older and more mature, having been co-captain of the voyage, advisor to Jason, and at times I believed the only sane man aboard. We all know what happened to Jason and that fleece and Medea.

Achilles was thirteen when he returned from Cheiron's training. I knew by then that he had seen his Mother often, since nearby was one of Her favorite spots to bathe with Her many sisters. And also She could not stay away from him. That would end up being Her tragedy: not that She'd been unable to make Achilles fully divine, but how little control She had over him, even with her Immortal love and powers of persuasion. She discovered what I'd known for years: he did whatever he wished.

We became friends afterward, Thetis and I, eventually. She had returned to the sea, and I suppose she had also returned to Zeus' couch. I had remarried a lovely young princess from another land named Electra — no, not that poor creature! It was a common name then. I was a father again, this time with a handful to play with, and I enjoyed fatherhood.

Achilles, my first son, returned to court and at first he brought me pride and pleasure. By thirteen he was already almost at his full height. He was thickly muscled. He could outrun any man we might set against him, having learned to race alongside fleet Cheiron, leagues at a time. His strength and prowess at arms was already legendary and he clearly was holding back whenever he "played" (his word) with the other elite soldiers.

Of course he was welcomed by the Myrmidons, for once gathered altogether in Phthia, as there were no wars for them to fight and I thought (hoped, I suppose) that surely one of that surly, masculine group would take him on as his *ephebe* to complete his training in becoming a man: to teach him affection and trust and loyalty and sensitivity to others. But that did not happen.

Achilles remained alone, apart. When I probed him, oh so gently, he said he was happy. He sometimes acted like an ordinary teenager, hiding himself in the women's quarters and then exploding out when they were all gathered together, revealing himself dressed in their clothing. He fathered a child with one girl, naturally the tomboy. But he never wed her, though he acknowledged the babe and adopted him. This infant would be named Pyrrhus, and would become our eventual heir.

To me he was distant, I who had been so very close to him! Had I not had the other children about me then I would have been more saddened. To others he was silent, polite, even courteous; but almost not present. I asked if he wanted to return to Cheiron. No. I asked if he wanted to go visit my hero companions in their homelands: he seemed to have enjoyed them so much. No, not really, no.

Every encounter I had with him, I came away with the oddest impression, as though Achilles was waiting for someone; Or waiting for something.

It turned out he was waiting for both.

First the "someone" came along. And then, not too far behind, the "something" arrived. The some-very-big-thing indeed -- a war with a thousand ships and four hundred thousand Achaean soldiers pitted against the strongest city of the time, peopled by fifty thousand, and with five hundred thousand allies. Now *that* was a stage large enough for Achilles to deign to act upon.

***

Oddly enough, Achilles was away when my fate -- and his -- arrived in Phthia.

I was atop the palace with the children that balmy afternoon watching the ship carrying him away to visit with my old companions, the Gemini. As its highest sail vanished from sight, headed south, a second craft hove into view from the east and headed straight into our little port.

I was about to drop down to my quarters for a summertime nap when my second-oldest son, Cleithes, a boy of five but with the sharpest sight said, "Look Sire. This boat flies with a small black sail. What does that mean?"

"Bad news," I said, and thinking aloud. "Possibly it reports that some friend or relative of mine has died."

Once down in the palace I had a courtier ride down to the harbor to find out who had landed and where that boat came from. The disturbance of seeing the black sail had bothered me too much for me to sleep.

Crepsis returned quickly enough. "The boat comes from Opuntian Locris. From King Menoetius, your kinsman. The main passenger is his second son, who is headed up to the palace now. I'll have quarters prepared for him and his companion.

Menoetius had been with me on the Argo and had been an attendant at the Calydonian Board Hunt. Why was he sending me his son?

The companion carried the winged scroll of a messenger and wore the winged sandals of a messenger. Despite the hot weather, his companion, the Prince, was dressed in garments down to his bare feet and almost covering his head. Sailors carried in a tripod of bronze with scenes etched into it that I recognized as from our trip together to the east. Also the gift of a gold ring with a golden stone embedded as big as a man's eye, called Topaz.

I'd set up a meeting out of doors in what little breeze we had, and sat there with my children at my feet and my queen at my side and my courtiers surrounding, and thus I suppose I felt in some way guarded from whatever bad news might be coming my way.

"Honored King Peleus, Protector of Emathia! Most Beloved of the First Born Son of Rhea!" the messenger began, in such old fashioned language that several courtiers tittered. "My lord, King Menoetius of Opus in Locris, begs you to accept a task only the most Godly may perform, and for which you are compensated greatly." His opening flourish done, he seemed self satisfied and took a draught of wine. But he also perspired and seemed nervous.

I thought I head the creature wrapped up in sea-stained linen snicker at his words. Perhaps not.

Holding his staff up, the messenger then explained that the young prince had committed an accidental assault upon his cousin, Clysonius, much beloved of the king, who had then died. King Menoetius was asking that the boy be taken to a temple, made to fast, do penitence, be cleansed of the sin by "One so close to Godhead that the ritual *must* be accepted."

He reminded me that Menoetius and my own father Aeacus shared a mother, Aegina. My grandsire was Zeus; his, the great King Actor: so we were cousins. He remembered at the end to introduce himself, a name I never recalled, and then named the Prince -- Patroclus.

"Prince Patroclus, cousin, take off your penitent garments." I said. "And drink this cooled wine."

How can one describe one's destiny? Once before it had arrived in the form of a goddess of the sea. And now, suddenly, in front of me, wearing a wrinkled royal *chiton*, with flushed face and perspiring skin, and eyes the same color as that great Topaz, it faced me once again. Patroclus was the youth of my dreams: he reminded me of my first love, my child brother Telamon, and of my second love, King – of this land, and of Thetis too, my third and greatest love. I must have made some noise from deep within, seeing him for the first time.

I spoke, "Prince Patroclus. Which God did this deed?"

He looked at the messenger, who looked back sternly.

"I alone am to blame."

I sent the messenger away, and asked the lad again.

"Lord Apollo, I believe," he answered this time, speaking freely. Perhaps in his land one must never place blame on the Olympians. "He has dogged my steps for these six moons past. He will not take no for an answer."

I could easily see why.

"Who is your *erasthes*? I asked. The boy was maybe sixteen at this time: slender, yet muscled as a young man is. "Did he not stand up for you?

"We do not follow that custom."

"Then the God thought you anyone's property," I explained. "The fault is your father's or your customs."

I agreed to have him put up, and his messenger too but in a chamber far away from him. I asked my chamberlain to arrange for the ritual to be performed that next day.

"The boy needs to do penance," he argued.

"How long have you been wrapped tight in those hot robes?" I asked. "What have you eaten since you left home?"

"Wrapped the three days it took to sail here. I ate only a handful of sunflower seeds and water each day," Patroclus answered. "Afraid I would become too ill from the choppy waves and lose face before you all."

I liked his pride. I declared the penance already done. Patroclus kissed my hand as I stood. I felt lightning jolt through my body. I would be his *erasthes*.

That night I told my wife my plan. She accepted it as a good wife would, and moved back to the women's quarters.

The ritual was held in the temple of Zeus and according to the priest all signs were that He accepted the cleansing. If only I knew then what more my ancestor-Lord had in store for me I wouldn't have been so elated.

We then walked barefoot, heads covered, to the temple of Apollo, where we made another sacrifice, and there before Apollo we declared ourselves *ephebe* and *erastes*.

And so I fell in love again.

***

Almost a year passed, perhaps the happiest of my life, because unlike with my Goddess-wife, I was never anxious, never felt unsure of my words or actions, never thought I must speak softly or keep my thoughts to myself. With Patroclus I was as though sixteen again myself, a decade ago. All that I had enjoyed, being *ephebe* to King Eurytion, I now enjoyed providing for my *ephebe*. We spent all our time together whether inside or out, summer, fall, winter, then spring and summer again. I sometimes wondered if I was now being compensated for my great loss and ire when my *erastes* was taken from me. Artemis had promised me a reward. Surely this lad was it.

Achilles returned taller, broader, more tan. He wore his hair long in a single braid as the Peloponnesians did, with ringlets on either side of his face, accenting his strong nose and perfect lips, and partly covering the corners of his long eyes, gray like his mother's. Everyone at court fell in love with him. Or so I was told. He asked to set up house between the palace and the Myrmidon's barracks and I gave leave, and had him helped to build it. He moved in his wife and toddler, and I was glad to see that he was taking his role as heir seriously, entertaining guests after they'd stopped into my court, having dinner parties with his own friends, usually other soldiers.

Patroclus had begged to be trained as a Myrmidon so he might return home eventually with double honor, and I wasn't always able to join him. So, I have to suppose that was where he and my son met. And continued to meet.

The Achaean peoples were in some motion at this time. Roads had become guarded and troublemakers dispatched and travel was thus safer. The improvements we'd made upon the Argo out of necessity on our long voyage now became common on all ships. King Agamemnon and his brother Menelaus had joined with other Kings to form a Southern Alliance and sent envoys with gifts and compliments to northern kingdoms like ours. I was kept busy with diplomacy, busy with guests from afar, busy trying to comprehend this new trend of unification, which felt somehow wrong.

That is the only reason I can provide for why I did not experience Patroclus' turn away from me. It wasn't until one day he left for the barracks and did not return at night that I realized it had happened. He returned the next day, with an excuse. But after a month, he did not return at all, and my courtiers fled from my approach out of fear that I'd ask them where he was.

At the home of Achilles, it turned out. This, my second oldest, Cleithes already knew, and he innocently told me.

"What does he do there?" I asked.

The boy shrugged. "Whatever men do," he answered, much of which was still baffling to him.

I invited Patroclus to a feast welcoming some Thessalians who had come with horses as I knew he admired horses and he arrived with Achilles and several Myrmidons. Their leader, Lynceus, took me aside to tell me the lad had begged admittance to their barracks.

I toyed with saying I had not yet renounced him as an *ephebe*, then seeing Lynceus' perspiration and obvious anxiety over having to ask me, I relented.

It proved the right move. Patroclus came to me, kissed me, thanked me and the next day he appeared in riding gear with his bow. We rode out that afternoon and the next.

At court he led only half a life: and young men get antsy. If I must, I would share him with the others. He sometimes stayed in my bed at night, although less and less often. I still hadn't understood what had happened.

The blood-red front sail of the two ship envoy from King Agamemnon arrived: Cotton-headed Thyestes, Wise handsome, old Nestor and Wily Odysseus invited Phthia to war upon Troy. The reason I'd already heard from others was given again, but I knew that booty and power were the real causes. I reminded the Ithacan con-artist that I was the progeny of Zeus and wed to a Goddess: No battle must touch my hands.

They feasted and went off next day to Achilles' house where they received a far warmer welcome. That had been the point, after all, to get the fearless shining one to join.

150

A day after their sails were gone from our port, headed to Euboea and then homeward, Lynceus came to court begging leave for himself and all the Myrmidons. They would leave with my first born son at their head, a hundred and ninety of them. They begged to borrow five of my ships besides their own two and I agreed. A contract was made specifying their return in one year with a particular value of treasure.

For the next few weeks, the capital, the center of my little kingdom, was alive with preparations for the war. It had become popular with the people and everyone aided those leaving and wished them well. Many individuals joined them in various camp-following capacities upon their ships.

I had awakened one night shortly after Lynceus's decision, to hear and then see Patroclus leave bed before dawn, which was not unusual. But he never returned and no messenger I sent to the barracks ever located him.

My chamberlain, Helops, was embarrassed when I asked where Patroclus was that no one could find him.

"All know he lives now with the Prince Achilles."

I waited until the night before they were to leave and then rode with a small party first to the barracks, and then to the Achilles' courtyard.

He was out of doors himself but the lad never came out of the house.

"He has left your palace of his own free will, Sire," were Achilles' first words to me, before even a greeting. A slap to my face. "He goes where I go now."

"To Troy? To die? For no good reason?" I asked.

"There are many good reasons."

"For you there may be. This war is Zeus' personal gift to you," I said. "He couldn't have done better by you, could He?"

"I am a soldier. A great field has opened," he admitted. He would not look me in the eye.

"What does your goddess-mother think of all this?"

"She does not approve. She has had the Immortal Goldsmith fashion shoes of thin silver for me, to protect my ankles; and forged gold and iron into armor and helmet."

"Then you will return safely," I acknowledged. "But why drag the boy along with you?"

"He's eighteen: a man. It's his wish."

"It's his passion. His and your unnatural passion for each other. This is not our custom, Achilles, as you know. The lover and the beloved must be of different generations for the relationship to be sanctified."

"All accept us," Achilles said. "All but the old."

At that moment I should have struck him, and should have been stuck dead in return, but Lynceus came between us. He bent upon a knee and he held my hand to keep it still, all but mewling on the ground there, in fear of what father and son would do to each other.

At last I said, "Bring Patroclus unharmed from Troy."

"I will bring him back unharmed."

Then, in my great anger and my utter despair, I said the fateful words I often wish had never left my mouth.

"Bring him back unharmed -- or do not return *at all!*"

Achilles' face went white.

"Swear it upon your great grandfather, Zeus Himself!" I demanded.

He stood fast. "I swear it upon Zeus Himself!"

"Achilles swore the oath," I said. "You are witness, Lynceus."

"Achilles swore the oath. I am witness!" Lynceus said, his tears flowing now.

"Achilles swore the oath. I am witness!" thundered a dozen Myrmidons who had surrounded us.

I whirled onto my horse and left.

***

They say that after Patroclus – dressed in Achilles' armor -- was killed by Hector, that my son went out on the field like a fury out of Hades' deepest chambers.

Lynceus reported that he witnessed my son slash the silver shoes Hephaestus had made with his sword beforehand, so that his ankles would be unprotected. In effect committing suicide: and fulfilling his oath to me.

On the fifth day of his non-stop killing spree, enraged Aphrodite guided Paris' arrow into Achilles' single vulnerable, bare heel.

As he bent to withdraw the arrow, ten Trojans brought him down and hacked him to pieces.

After his death, the Myrmidons returned home to Phthia. They didn't remain for the sack of the city.

For this, they were honored and remained safe. Recall that all the other Achaeans who took part in that wanton destruction ended up paying some kind of high price: Agamemnon paid with his life.

After my grief had abated a little, I caused to be erected a temple to the memory of Patroclus. I called in a sculptor to make his likeness, and directed him daily until it looked just like him the last time I saw him. Then it was cast in bronze and put up. For over a decade of war, the Myrmidons had returned with much Asian treasure. They provided the gold leaf that would cover his head and his hands and his lovely feet.

The dedication of that temple was the last great celebration in Phthia that I presided over as king.

In later generations, people came to believe that it was a temple not to love but to war: to the shining one.

His half-destroyed silver shoes had been returned to us after Troy fell, snatched by his son Pyrrhus from Priam's treasure room.

Later on, these shoes were placed under the statue's feet. For centuries, sacrifices were made to this supposed statue of Achilles, by soldiers going to war and by pairs of male lovers.

Felice Picano

is the author of twenty-five books of poetry, fiction, memoirs, and nonfiction. His work is translated into fifteen languages. Several titles were national and international bestsellers; four plays have been produced. He's considered a founder of modern gay literature along with other members of the Violet Quill. His most recent work is *True Stories: Portraits From My Past (2011) Contemporary Gay Romances (2011),* and *Twelve O'Clock Tales (2012.* Find his stories, essays, and reviews at www.felicepicano.net

A Charming Menage

Ann Herendeen

Prince Charming had a problem. "I'm shooting blanks," he whispered to his boyfriend, Anthony, late one night after a very long state dinner with too many toasts had made him careless.

"That's a relief," Anthony said. "I'm not ready to have kids. Or are you just saying that so I'll let you bareback me?"

"No, seriously," Rupert said. ("Charming" is a courtesy title, like Dauphin in ancien-régime France.) "I'm twenty-five and I've never fathered a child."

"Maybe," Anthony said, "you have to have sex with a woman first."

Rupert hit Anthony with his pillow, Anthony retaliated with his pillow, and following a rather giggly, groggy wrestling session, there were, after all, one or two instances of barebacking that night. But this was a mythical kingdom; sexually-transmitted diseases did not exist, so no harm done.

Later that morning Rupert was still brooding. "You know I'm bisexual, right?"

"I just thought it's what you told the 'rents so they'd leave us alone," Anthony said. (Mythical kingdoms tend to have a time-lag when it comes to slang.)

"You don't give them enough credit. My dad's bi, too. He and the Royal Gamekeeper are always going off on these private 'hunting trips.'

And Mom—she's had 'things' with her ladies-in-waiting as far back as I can remember."

"TMI," Anthony said. "So, when do I meet the little wife?"

"That's the problem," Rupert said. "I can't get married until I prove I can carry on the ancestral line. And I've been of age for four years now and not one girl has claimed I'm her baby daddy."

"When do you have time to be with girls anyway? I've never seen you with a girl, not since, what was her name? The one with all the hair."

"Rapunzel," Rupert said, laughing. "Boy, talk about high maintenance. No, it's civics class."

"You lost me," Anthony said.

"Come on. You don't really think I need three entire afternoons a week to learn the governing principles of a principality smaller than Lichtenstein and with a wizard, a grand vizier and a prime minister to run things?"

"You mean--"

"Yeah. Three different girls each 'class.' Sometimes four."

"You poor thing," Anthony said. "No wonder you're always tired on—" He thought back over the years. "—Monday, Wednesday and Friday nights."

Rupert got a dreamy expression on his face. "It's actually kind of fun. Or at least it was. But now I feel so—impotent."

"Poor baby. Don't think like that. Maybe they're using birth control. Maybe they don't want to get pregnant from a few sordid sessions with the prince—no offense, honey."

"You are such a cunt," Rupert said, but affectionately. "It's not that sordid. And the whole point of it is that if I knock a girl up and the kid's healthy, I'll marry her. So they have an incentive. And there hasn't been one credible claim. Nobody's even tried."

"That's bizarre," Anthony said. "How can you be sure?"

"See, they stay in a special dormitory. No men allowed within a mile of the place, until they get their monthly bleed. After I've been with them a few times they stay another month or two, so they can't pass someone else's brat off as mine and—"

"Nothing?"

"Nothing."

Cinderella had a problem. "I want to go to Prince Charming's civics class," she told her stepsister Adrienne, the nice one. Sure, she was ugly, but she was not at all wicked. Or at least only in bed, where it was an advantage.

"Oh, sweetie," Adrienne said. "I'm sorry."

"Why can't I go?" Emily said. ("Cinderella" is, obviously, a pen name.) "Every other girl has."

Adrienne thought before answering—a rare quality in anyone under sixty. "If it helps," she said, "you're not missing anything."

"Liar," Emily said. "You said he was gorgeous. And kind. And sexy. I was right there in the kitchen when you told us."

"He is. But I mean the whole experience. It's so degrading. You have to stay in this fleabag dormitory, no separate rooms. It's like joining some weird convent, but without the fun parts. Everyone's so focused on getting pregnant they don't want to jinx it by having girl sex. Then you're ushered into the Royal Bedchamber, and after an hour that's it, put your clothes on and back to Motel 6. You can't take a shower, in case you wash away the 'royal seed.' And it's not even a full hour, because the prince has to have time to get it up for the next girl."

"So why did you go?" Emily said. "If it's so degrading."

"Because he's Prince Charming, of course," Adrienne said. "If I'd gotten pregnant I'd be his consort. When he is King, dilly-dilly, I shall be Queen."

"But you didn't."

"No."

"And neither did Sylvia."

"Thank God," Adrienne said. "She's my sister and I love her, but if that bitch ever became the boss of me, I'd kill myself."

"So why shouldn't I try?"

Adrienne sighed. "You're going to make me say it, aren't you? Because you can't have children. That's why your father favors me and Sylvia over you, so there'll be a next generation to inherit." After a long, horrible silence, she whispered, "I'm sorry."

Emily sat up. "How do you know? How do you know I can't have kids?"

"Shhh," Adrienne said, hugging Emily, kissing her and stroking her face to calm her. "Because you're, you know, sort of in-between. You don't have breasts, and you don't bleed."

"But--"

"Look on the bright side. You can mess around with anybody and never get in trouble."

"I don't want anybody," Emily said. "The only one I want is you."

"Me too," Adrienne said. They shared a much more passionate kiss this time, which led to stroking of more than just the face, and some heavy breathing and moaning.

In fact Sylvia, trying to sleep in the next room, had to bang on the wall several times because of the screaming. "If you don't stop, I'll tell Dad," she shouted.

"Go ahead," Emily said. "He's not your real father anyway."

"I'll tell Mom," Sylvia said. "Then you'll get in trouble. You're just a lesbo because you're not a real woman and men don't want you."

"And nobody wants you," Adrienne said, "because you're nasty."

In the morning, as she was serving breakfast, Emily said, "I don't see why I can't go to civics class."

"Because I'll tell," Sylvia said. "I'll tell everybody what you are." She glared at her step sibling, with her shining beauty that filthy rags and kitchen chores could not extinguish, and was consumed with jealousy that she was Adrienne's friend and not hers. "Unless…"

And that's how Emily ended up sleeping with both her stepsisters. Not at the same time, of course. Unlike Adrienne, who enjoyed taking turns, Sylvia made Emily do all the work. Still, it was an education.

Anthony had a problem. He had tried to be cool after learning about the "civics classes," but the idea bothered him. Not so much that Rupert had been having regular hetero sessions every week for years without telling him—not that that was so heartwarming, either—but that he enjoyed it.

"I thought," he would say, and always swallowed the rest of the sentence. For days, Anthony caught himself on the verge of saying to Rupert, "I thought you loved me," and for days he stopped after two words.

"What?" Rupert demanded, as they sat side by side at another of those interminable state dinners. "What did you think? For God's sake, honey, just say it!"

"I thought—I thought—" Anthony took a deep breath. "I thought, why don't we get married, you and me, and—"

Rupert laughed. The tension left his face and he let the air out of his lungs, as if he'd been holding his breath for a week. "I thought you'd never ask." He banged his fist on the table until people stopped talking (it was a mythical kingdom, but not entirely civilized), and said, "I have an announcement."

At his father's nod, Rupert stood up, pulled Anthony to stand beside him, raised their clasped hands over their heads and said, "Anthony Edouard Francis Mallon, Marquess of Westwood, Viscount D'Aubigny, Baron Rezniak, son and heir to our esteemed Chancellor (the kingdom had one of those, too), Lothar, Duke of Langdale, Earl of—"

Anthony nudged Rupert in the ribs. "Get on with it."

Rupert nudged Anthony back, cleared his throat and said in his parade-ground voice, the one he used when commanding the Household Cavalry, "Lord Westwood has made me an honorable proposal of marriage, and I have accepted."

Everybody cheered. The men whistled and stamped their feet, and the women made that scary ululating sound like women in Middle Eastern countries. (This mythical kingdom wasn't in the Middle East, but it had some far-reaching trade agreements, so there was a lot of cultural exchange.)

Once he could be heard above the bawdy singing and the raunchy shouted good wishes, the King said, "Technically, Rupert is supposed to be the one who asks, but We've been waiting so long for this, We're not going to quibble."

"No, indeed," the Queen said. She winked at her husband. "We'd better post a new broadsheet."

The King shook Anthony's hand. "Welcome to the family. The Mallons have always served Us well. Your father and I have hoped for this day ever since you and Rupert were pages together."

The Queen was eyeing Anthony in a peculiar way. "I do hope you'll learn to like snails," she said. "The Prince's consort must enjoy both, you know. Snails and oysters."

The next day was Friday. After the morning routine: military drill, sitting in on the King's public audience, and a visit to a charity for the chronically homophobic, Rupert kissed his fiancé on the lips and said, "Good luck. I'll save you a plate of oysters for dinner. You'll need them."

"What are you talking about?" Anthony said.

"What do you think?" Rupert said. "Civics class."

Anthony shook his head. "I thought we were getting married. Or didn't 'yes' mean yes last night? It sure felt like yes when you gave me the best blow job of—"

"You don't have to shout," Rupert said, peering over his shoulders like a commoner, as if he cared whether someone overheard. "Would you like me to come with you?"

"Come with me where?"

"To civics class. It's your turn now."

Anthony stepped back several paces. "Are you out of your mind?"

"I'm perfectly sane," Rupert said, "but you seem a little agitated. Which is why I thought I'd come with you for the first couple of sessions."

"That's disgusting."

Rupert raised his eyebrows and looked down his long, shapely royal nose. "What did you say?"

"You heard me," Anthony said. "And don't go all lèse majesté on me. I've known you too long for that."

"You think I'm disgusting?"

Anthony rolled his eyes. "Do I have to spell it out? OK. Here's what's disgusting: You plowing your way through every slut in the kingdom, behind my back, all the time we've been together. You expecting me to do the ones you didn't manage to get to. And you want to know what's really disgusting? Your pornographic three-way fantasy. I had no idea you were such a sicko."

"If I'm a sicko, you're a prude," Rupert said." And they're not sluts. They're nice girls, most of them. And I don't want a three-way, you pervert. I thought you might need help getting started—"

Anthony punched Rupert hard in the face, wincing as he saw Rupert's magnificent nose mashed to one side and gushing blood. "Oh, God, honey, I'm sorry. I just don't understand—" He ran to help his lover, directly into the arms of a squadron of Royal Guards, who hauled him away to the dungeon. Even a fiancé of noble lineage is not allowed to assault a member of the royal family.

"You shouldn't have hit me," Rupert said. "At least not in public." He looked tired, and the large bandage over his broken nose only added to the pathetic effect.

Anthony attempted a smile. "I'll remember that. The next time you want to have a bisexual three-way, I'll wait until we're alone before I beat the crap out of you."

"That's the spirit," Rupert said.

"Is your nose going to be OK?"

"No. I mean yes. It's no big deal. But I'll never win a beauty contest now."

"A dream denied is a terrible thing."

"Unfeeling brute."

"So," Anthony said, after the silence threatened to last all night, "who do I have to fuck to get out of this cell?"

"Me," Rupert said, smiling. He stuck his arm through the bars.

Anthony took Rupert's hand and kissed it. "I can handle that."

Rupert pulled his hand away. "And some girls."

"Not that again," Anthony said. "Whatever you need me to do, kiss your ass on the palace balcony or spend a day in the pillory, I'll do it."

"Don't be so melodramatic. Everybody knows lovers have lovers' quarrels. I've already promised Dad you won't do it again, and that's that. He and Mom are crazy about you. But you have to stop overreacting to this business with the girls."

" 'Overreacting?' I'm not overreacting. I'm gay."

"So what? I'm not asking you to fall in love. Hell, I'm not even asking you to marry a girl. Just fuck a few so I can have an heir."

Anthony thought he was going to faint, or be sick, which feels very much the same. He sank down on the narrow wooden plank that served as a bed and lowered his head between his knees.

Rupert squatted on his haunches, peering through the gloom, so that his face was on the same level as Anthony's. "Honey? Are you all right?" His voice rose to a hysterical shriek. "Did those bastards beat you? Because if they did, I will personally put them on the rack and—"

Anthony lifted his head with an immense effort. "Stop it, Rupert. Nobody beat me."

"Then what's wrong?"

"You," Anthony said. "You're scaring me with all this crazy talk about girls and heirs."

Rupert had a moment of insight. "Haven't you ever made love with a girl before?"

"No, you asshole. I'm gay, remember?"

"But, but." Rupert was at a loss. "Didn't you ever, you know, experiment? To find out what it's like?"

"No," Anthony said. "I never ate a cockroach, or drove a nine-inch nail into my skull or drank drain cleaner. I didn't feel the need to experiment with those things either."

Rupert laughed. "I can safely promise you that having sex with a woman is a lot better than drinking drain cleaner."

"Oh yes? But what about cockroaches and nails?"

"Are you worried that you won't be able to? Just because you've never tried doesn't mean you can't—" Rupert searched for a delicate way to say it. "—perform with a woman."

"You want to watch me 'perform' with one of your bimbos?" Anthony said. "Maybe I'm better off rotting away in this dungeon."

Rupert groaned. "I thought you knew. When I told you I'm shooting blanks, and then you proposed. What do you think it means, for crying out loud, to marry Prince Charming?"

Anthony had no answer. He sat, his elbows on his thighs, hands propping up his head that seemed to weigh a ton, and watched Rupert out of the corners of his eyes.

"It means," Rupert said, "that if I can't beget an heir, and since I don't have brothers or sisters, my partner will father the child in my place. That's you, honey. That's what you proposed and I accepted."

"But I didn't," Anthony said. "All I did was ask you to marry me. You and me."

"And what about kids? How did you propose to solve that?"

Anthony shrugged. "Adoption. I don't know."

"Where do you think we are?" Rupert said. "San Francisco? New York? This is here. East of the Sun and West of the Moon. Fairy Land. Mother Goose's Neighborhood. My kingdom, or it will be. And I need someone to inherit after me."

"I'm sorry," Anthony said. "I didn't think." Every family with property or land or money to pass down to the next generation wanted a blood relative. (It was a medieval point of view, but this was, as I've

161

mentioned, a mythical kingdom, and unavoidably medieval in many ways.) "I'm lucky. I come from a large family, and I just didn't think."

"No. That's all right. I'm glad we've sorted this out."

"Have we?"

"We can still make the second sitting for dinner." Rupert snapped his fingers and a guard unlocked the cell door. "I've saved you a whole barrel of oysters. We'll take it easy this weekend. Then on Monday you'll start civics class."

Anthony fainted into Rupert's arms.

Emily saw the announcement of the Prince's engagement on the message board at the market on Monday morning. Next to it was a flier for advanced civics classes, an intense course, just three weeks, no dormitory residence required. Girls who had taken the first class were still eligible to attend, and any new girls who hadn't yet studied civics were particularly welcome. In a month there would be a ball to celebrate the Prince's weddings.

Most people in the kingdom were illiterate; they got their news from heralds, town criers and gossip. But the royal family felt it couldn't hurt to put the notices in writing as well. Brought in a better class of girls, the Queen said.

Emily had been educated at home before her mother died, and she enjoyed catching the early edition on market days. She studied the color portraits on the broadsheet, the broad-shouldered, golden-haired prince and the slender, dark-haired fiancé with the perfect profile, and checked the flier again. "Weddings," it said. Plural.

The sundial in the square was showing a shadow—past sunrise. Emily barely had time to do her errands and get home to make breakfast, but she had to risk it. She turned away from the farmers' market and the grocers' shops, into a narrow, dark street, walking by instinct and memory until she stood in front of her godmother's door.

The old woman stared up at the gangly youth in tattered dress and soiled apron. "What do you want—Emily? How you've grown! But I'd know that face anywhere, the image of your dear mama. Come in, come in. Now, tell me what's troubling you."

"Oh, Godmother," Emily said, "I want to go to the Prince's civics classes. But they'll never let me in looking like this."

The Good Witch (what else could she be? She had a certificate signed by Glinda herself) led Emily through the kitchen and out into the overgrown backyard, talking more to herself than to her goddaughter. "What shall it be, skirts or breeches? Ah, yes, I see." With a flick of the wrist and a touch of her long staff, she created a gossamer gown from cabbage leaves and spiders' webs still sparkling with dew. She turned pieces of gravel into a necklace and earrings of seed pearls, and used the fur from an inquisitive squirrel to trim a pair of strappy, high-heeled sandals.

"Don't stay longer than an hour," she said, wrapping the fine things in a soiled sheet for safekeeping and cackling at her own cleverness. "It all changes back, you know."

Anthony waited in the Royal Bedchamber, the one he shared with Rupert. He was sweating so heavily he could smell himself. He tried to remember another time he'd been so nervous, but even that final battle with the Rumplestiltskin forces hadn't been as scary as this. Warfare was his profession, after all. As the eldest son of the Chancellor, he was entitled to the position of Major General. He'd trained for it since childhood and he had a good head for tactics. If he had to cleave a few Stiltskins in half with the broadsword, so much the better. It had been a gory victory, but a victory nonetheless.

Whereas this—this was the downside of warfare: long stretches of boredom punctuated by brief moments of terror. A broadsword and chainmail were no help at all.

There was a knock on the door and one of the Queen's ladies introduced the first girl. "This is Adrienne, my lord. Adrienne, you'll be with Lord Westwood today."

Anthony's stomach lurched. The girl was hideous. She couldn't help it, poor thing, but she had a lumpy figure cinched tightly into a frilly dress, like a muslin sack filled with rutabagas and tied with a lace ribbon. Her features were coarse, with a unibrow over close-set eyes, a blob of a nose, and thin lips that inadequately concealed a snaggletooth jaw.

Adrienne eyed Anthony from across the room, a truculent expression on her face. "You're not Prince Charming."

"No," Anthony said. "I'm Lord Westwood, the Prince's fiancé. But call me Anthony, please." He smiled, what had always been one of his assets. But now he could feel his mouth doing odd things, twitching and grimacing.

"What's the matter with you?" Adrienne said. "You look like you swallowed a cockroach."

"Drain cleaner, actually," Anthony muttered.

"Last time I was with Prince Charming," Adrienne said. "And he behaved like a perfect gentleman."

Fortunately Adrienne decided she wasn't interested in repeating any civics lessons with an inferior teacher. She slammed out the door before Anthony could think of a courteous way of saying he was indisposed.

The door opened again immediately. "All done with Adrienne?" the Queen's lady inquired as she ushered in the next candidate, Sylvia.

Anthony thought he was going to have a heart attack. There was an unmistakable and horrifying family resemblance, but Sylvia looked, if possible, uglier than Adrienne, and her demeanor seemed, if anything, less agreeable. He tried to gather what remained of his wits, remembering battlefield tactics. If all seems lost, create a diversion.

"Would you like a glass of wine?" He pointed to the bottle of fine burgundy on the table.

Sylvia made a hawking noise. She actually spat, a big gob of phlegm that missed Anthony's over-the-knee suede boots by less than an inch. "Fuck that," she said. "Stand and deliver, boyfriend." She pulled her dress over her head, revealing enormous, sagging breasts bursting out of a straining corset held together with knotted string, and a bulging stomach that could have concealed, by Anthony's estimate, two or three pregnancies with no one the wiser.

The woman advanced on him, grinning and holding out her arms.

Anthony felt his legs buckling. He collapsed onto the bed and, for the second time in his life, fainted.

When he woke up the Queen's lady was leaning over him, laying a wet handkerchief on his forehead.

"Can't you do a better job of vetting them?" Anthony said.

"It is not my place," the woman said, nose in the air. "All I do is check the list and mind the door. If Lord Westwood is recovered, I will send in the next one."

So it went, for three hours. There were a couple of nice, pretty girls, but most of them were hard cases: prostitutes, penniless widows, single mothers with large broods from multiple fathers, weathered farm laborers—all looking for a way out of poverty and hopelessness.

Anthony couldn't imagine having sex with any of them. The decent prospects were so few and far between, by the time one of them came along he was too frazzled to try. Most of them he sent out after a minute or two of suspicious conversation on both sides. With the better sorts he offered a glass of wine, hoping to gain some false courage. Sometimes they accepted, but only to be polite.

"I'm sorry, my lord," said a refined young woman who had given her name as Snow White, "but the reason we're all here is that we thought we'd be hooking up with Prince Charming. You're a very pleasant young man, but—" She took a ladylike sip of wine, stood up and opened the door. "It's false advertising, you know."

By the end of the afternoon, Anthony was exhausted. He'd never felt so defeated in his life, not even during that disastrous retreat when the Pied Piper's Rat Army, led by the infamous Puss in Boots, had made a predawn incursion on the northern border. At least Anthony had managed to bring his own regiment home more or less intact.

He looked up. A tall girl had slipped in silently and was staring down at him where he sat slumped at the table, a sympathetic expression on her face.

"I suppose you're worn out by now," she said. "Even the Prince didn't get through so many girls in one day, or so I heard."

She was very pretty, with warm brown eyes fringed by long, lush eyelashes and a wide, kissable mouth. A diaphanous gown of pale green and white accentuated her boyish figure: flat chest, slim waist and narrow hips over long, slender legs. There was a modest pearl choker around her throat and matching drops in her ears. Her contralto voice was slightly husky, both ladylike and sensual.

If only she'd been the first one, Anthony thought, he might have been able to rise to the occasion. "Would you like a glass of wine?" he asked.

"Yes, please." She sat down on the other chair. "I was worried it would be wham, bam, thank you ma'am, without exchanging a word."

Anthony's hands were steady as he poured. "You did not attend the Prince's class?"

"No." She raised the glass in a toast. "Congratulations on your engagement."

"Thank you," Anthony said. "You're the first one to say it. Are you disappointed that I'm not him?"

"Not at all," the girl said. "I followed the entire Rumplestiltskin campaign in the broadsheets. You're quite a hero."

They spent the requisite hour together, talking and finishing the bottle. The girl was up on recent history and current events, and carried on a conversation like an educated person. She reminded Anthony of the aristocratic ladies who ran salons, where wit and sophistication ruled, and a man's title meant nothing if his manners were coarse or he was inarticulate.

When the Queen's lady knocked on the door, the girl stood up with a start and rushed out before Anthony had a chance to ask her name.

The woman consulted her list, holding the parchment up to the light and singeing the edge on the torch in the wall sconce. "Hmm. I can't make it out. Cindy? Cellar? Cenerentola?"

Anthony snorted. "Anyway, can you find out who she is and have her come back?"

"Of course, my lord," the woman said, frowning at the impossible task.

"And next time, put her first."

"So, how did it go?" Rupert asked that night, draping his arm along Anthony's shoulders. "I heard you really hit it off with the last one."

Anthony removed Rupert's arm and staggered to the bed. "Horrible. The last girl was lovely, but you can't imagine the succession of whores, pigs, sluts and frights that preceded her."

"Don't be such a fag," Rupert said.

"I am a fag," Anthony said. "If you weren't such an asshole, you wouldn't make me go through with this."

"I'm sorry." Rupert lay down beside Anthony and tried to kiss him.

Anthony turned his head away. "And if you ever call me a fag again, I'll knock you into the middle of Middle Earth and go to the gallows with no regrets."

"With your rank, it's the guillotine for you, my dear. Non, je ne regrette rien," Rupert sang off-key in a guttural voice.

Anthony booed like at the opera. "As a singer, you suck."

"You wish," Rupert said. "I bet you could use a suck right now."

"I'll say. My little sparrow."

Emily's stepsisters regaled her with their bad luck as she prepared supper. "That fiancé thinks he's God's gift but he can't even get it up," Sylvia said.

"And we can't put our names down again," Adrienne said. "They're giving priority to girls who haven't been before."

"Maybe I could go," Emily said in a small voice.

"Yeah, you'd go right to the top of the list," Sylvia said. "The D list."

"Why shouldn't Emily try?" Adrienne said. "It's not like it's Prince Charming."

"Maybe he's nice, the fiancé," Emily said.

"Maybe he's shooting blanks, Prince Charming," Sylvia said.

Emily's godmother couldn't get her on the list again until the following week, penciled into the last slot of a full day's program. When Anthony saw her, at the end of a long, miserable Monday afternoon, he almost wept with pleasure. "I thought you weren't coming."

"It's not easy to get on that list," Emily said. "You have to know somebody."

"I'll fix it," Anthony said. "I know somebody."

They both laughed.

Anthony had never felt so comfortable with a girl. Being with her was better than one of those salon ladies, more like an old friend. Almost like being with Rupert. He could seriously think about doing it with this one, whatever her name was.

"What's your--"

"Do you have any more of that wine?" Emily said. "And I meant to ask—that time when the Rat Army invaded didn't seem very well managed. Or don't you want to talk about it?"

"I was never so scared in my life," Anthony said. "It was my first command. I was only eighteen, and..." He had never told anyone about this failed campaign, not even Rupert, as the King was the Commander in

Chief and criticism was treason. But with this anonymous girl, he felt safe.

Emily leaned back against the pillows on the bed, listening and watching. When Anthony spoke, he became animated and excited. His languid, weary air evaporated as he talked openly and honestly about battle fatigue, the responsibilities of command and the cruelties inflicted on the countryside by the brutal warlord Puss in Boots.

The knock on the door came in the nick of time. Emily could feel her dress wilting like stale cabbage, floating away like dried cobwebs, the pearls losing their luster. Anthony tried to grab her hand, but she was too quick.

"Damn it," Anthony said as she fled down the hall. "There's less than a week to go. Please reschedule her, ASAP."

The Queen's lady squinted at the illegible scrawl. "Aschenputtel? That can't be right. Sounds German." Someone was being bribed to put false names on the list, and she didn't intend to let any more of that money escape.

"Where the hell have you been?" Sylvia said when Emily crept in late, tipsy and humming to herself. "The house is a pigsty, there's nothing to eat and my best gown is dirty."

"I'm sorry," Emily said. "I was--"

"Let me guess. Fucking the Prince's fiancé."

"Oh no. How would I get on the list?"

"It was a joke, you stupid bitch. Now, I want supper on the table, I want my gown cleaned and pressed, and I want this whole house put in order. Right now."

"Did you hear?" Adrienne ran into the room waving a broadsheet. "Prince Charming's ball is next week. He and Lord Westwood are celebrating their engagement, and then they're going to choose a wife."

"You mean for both of them?" Emily asked.

"No, dumbass," Sylvia said. "For the Prince. He's marrying Lord Westwood for love, but he needs a wife to have children."

"And we're all invited," Adrienne said. "Everybody. Including you, Emily."

"Very funny," Sylvia said. "Who'd want to marry her? She's not even really a woman."

"It's better this way," Rupert said. "I shouldn't have put you through those ridiculous civics classes."

"Now you tell me," Anthony said. "But there was one girl. If I have to do this, I'd choose her."

"That's fine," Rupert said. "We'll announce our betrothal at the beginning of the ball. Then you point her out and I'll talk to her, maybe dance once or twice. I'm not as picky as you. If you like her, I'm sure I can live with her. You're the one who has to do the work anyway. Problem solved."

"Not entirely," Anthony said. "I never could catch her name. I don't even know if she's from a decent family."

"Wow! You really went at it," Rupert said, a note of awe in his voice. "Don't worry. As long as she's under thirty, that's all that matters. And no, I'm sorry, but you can't wear chainmail. It's not that kind of ball."

Emily thought she wasn't going to make it to the ball, as her godmother fussed over so many garbled spells. "Eye of newt and toe of frog? No, that's not it. Fur of bat and—something of dog? Snakes and snails and puppy-dogs' tails? Why do I keep thinking of dogs? I wish I could remember where I'd left the recipe book."

At last Emily was dressed: a creamy white spider-silk shirt open at the neck, hip-hugging lizard-skin pants and flawless diamonds glinting at throat and ears. Her hair was washed in pure rainwater, cropped short to show off copper and bronze highlights. The only accessory that didn't match was the shoes, clear glass slides with kitten heels. "You mustn't be taller than he is," her godmother said. "Men don't like it."

"Can't I have some black leather ankle boots?" Emily asked. "They'd go better."

"No, dear," her godmother said. "It's the rules. You'd never slip out of a boot. I could trim them with squirrel fur again if you like."

Emily heard the town crier calling ten. "There's no time. Thank you, Godmother." She ran out to the waiting stretch limo, purple-black finish with palest green interior, and the surly rat driver sped off.

"Don't forget!" the witch called after her. "Not a moment past midnight!"

It struck Emily as she made her entrance that she was the only girl in pants. She hadn't questioned her godmother at the time—the clothes felt so natural. Now here she was, the lone butch in a roomful of busty, curvaceous, wide-hipped femmes, their long hair shaped into elaborate coiffures or hanging down in shimmering waves.

She saw Adrienne and Sylvia and made an about-face, but not quickly enough. "I'm free for the next dance," Adrienne said, standing in her path and simpering.

Emily shook her head.

"Oh, come on," Sylvia said. "You're a good-looking fella. The Prince is only going to pick one girl. The rest of us might as well have some fun."

Emily was tempted to dance with Adrienne, but knew better than to risk exposure. "I beg your pardon, ladies," she said, "but I am engaged for this dance. Perhaps the next one." She bowed and headed toward the front of the room.

"What lovely manners," Adrienne said.

Sylvia spat. "Just once," she said, "I'd like to meet a man who can do more than talk."

By the time Emily appeared Anthony had almost given up. Every girl in the kingdom was at the ball, and he had to dance with most of them. "You can keep an eye out for your 'soul mate,' " Rupert said, "and still look like you're giving each of them a fair shot."

The slim figure in the tailored shirt and pants shone as if haloed in moonlight as she glided through the dancing throng. Anthony dropped his dance partner's hands a beat before the music ended. "I was afraid I'd missed you."

"So, you're the one who has captivated my fiancé," Rupert said, appearing at Anthony's discreet signal. "I can't say I'm altogether surprised." He bowed very correctly, asked if Emily would excuse the two men for a moment and took Anthony aside.

"Did you think I wouldn't notice?" Rupert said. His voice was loud in the expectant hush. "You were supposed to choose a woman."

Emily felt tears forming in her eyes. Everybody was staring at her, all the girls and their anxious parents. The entire population of the kingdom was crammed into this one overheated, airless room and they were not going to be happy that Emily had been chosen over their daughters, especially when it turned out she wasn't even a woman…

Anthony turned his back on Rupert and stormed over to Emily. He put his hand under her chin and forced her face up. "Please don't cry."

"The Prince is right," Emily said. "I'm not exactly a woman."

"The Prince can be a real jerk sometimes," Anthony said. "True beauty has no gender." He took Emily's hand and swept her into a waltz before she could say no. They swirled around the room, alone at first, soon joined by dozens of other couples.

The music never stopped, just changed tempo. Anthony and Emily finished the waltz, then rumbaed, hustled, fox-trotted and slow-danced. After an hour or so their bodies were pressed together full-length, Emily's cheek resting on Anthony's shoulder, his hands gripping her butt, hers linked around his waist. Whatever she is, girl or boy, Anthony thought, she feels right for me. And he knew, whatever she was, he loved her.

This was heaven, Emily thought, leaning into Anthony's hard body. She let her hands drift lower, from Anthony's waist, to his hips…

When the chimes sounded for midnight Emily panicked.

"I'm sorry," she said. She yanked herself out of Anthony's embrace and dashed through the doors and down the steps so fast, the slippers flew off her feet. She snatched up the closer one and jumped into the waiting limo. But it was only an eggplant now, withered and imploding, with an enormous rat gnawing at the bulb end. The lizard-skin slithered off her hips like a used condom and she sprinted toward home, a scruffy lad in ragged shirt and breeches with a girl's sandal bulging in his pocket.

"Well, you certainly made a mess of that," Rupert said, as the last guests straggled out.

"Me?" Anthony said. He cradled the size-11 sandal like a bouquet of flowers. "You were the one forcing me into unnatural acts."

"Never mind. For all we know, you could be shooting blanks too. Let's get married, and we'll worry about having children later."

"No," Anthony said, "I love her. Him. Whatever. Not the way I love you, but it's love. And if I can't find her—him—the wedding's off."

"Now who's into kinky three-ways," Rupert said.

They didn't speak for a week.

But as Anthony persisted in the search, Rupert agreed to help. "I love you. Only you. If finding this person is what it takes for you to marry me, I'll find him—her."

Adrienne and Sylvia curled their hair and put on their best gowns every morning for weeks before the searchers reached their house. The two men were tired and dispirited. Rupert took a look at Adrienne and perked up. "I remember you from civics class."

"Will you be serious?" Anthony said.

"I am serious," Rupert said. "I've given up civics classes, not women. And I want a wife."

"But her?" Anthony shuddered. "I can't."

"You won't have to," Rupert said. "But it's only fair, if you find your—person, I should have someone too. Miss— Adrienne? Beautiful name. I apologize for my fiancé's behavior. He's going through a rough patch. Listen, Adrienne, do you know a sort of androgynous young man —"

A beautiful youth emerged from the kitchen wearing a white silk mini-dress over black lizard-skin tights, diamond studs in his ears, and carrying one glass sandal. He took the mate from Anthony and put them on, standing face to face, eye to eye, until Anthony kissed him on the lips.

"Would you mind very much being Lady Westwood instead of Princess Charming?" Anthony asked.

"I'd like that more than anything," Emily said. "But I can't even figure out if I'm Emily or Emile. And I don't want to leave Adrienne."

"That should not be a problem," Anthony said. "And please, don't choose one or the other. I love both of you. All of you."

"You see," Rupert was explaining to Emily's father and stepmother, "I like a woman with some meat on her bones, and Adrienne is good-natured and lusty in bed, as I recall. And neither of us is going to win any beauty contests."

A month after the royal wedding, Rupert married Adrienne in a private ceremony and Emile-Emily became Emilie, Lord Westwood's official consort.

When Rupert and Anthony were away on hunting trips or off at war, Emilie and Adrienne shared the Royal Bed. Adrienne was so happy she had become beautiful, her unibrow giving her the look of a voluptuous Frida Kahlo. Being in-laws was much better than being stepsisters, Emilie thought. Not only could they fool around and not get in trouble, it was a wifely duty. "Keep the bed warm for us," their husbands said with a wink as they set out on their manly adventures.

Sylvia inherited her stepfather's property, managed it well, and made an excellent marriage to an indulgent, deaf old duke. Whether her children were his, no one had the nerve to ask.

Rupert and Anthony adopted eventually. Customs must change with the times, Rupert declared, even in a mythical kingdom. Their son was somewhat feral, the result of Red Riding Hood's less fortunate encounter with a wolf when she was no longer little. Years later, during the Three Pigs real estate scam, the young Prince Charming saved the kingdom by blowing the overpriced houses down.

And they all lived happily ever after.

Ann Herendeen

Ann Herendeen writes from the "third perspective," the woman married to a bisexual husband and living in an m/m/f ménage. She is the author of two Harper Paperbacks: *Phyllida and the Brotherhood of Philander*; and *Pride/Prejudice*, a finalist for the Lambda Literary Award for Bisexual Fiction; and an e-book series: *Eclipsis, or Lady Amalie's memoirs*. Her third novel, *Last Dance* (in progress), also reworks the Cinderella story. www.annherendeen.com

About Gay City Health Project

Gay City Health Project has been providing innovative, community-driven HIV prevention and health promotion initiatives since 1995. Born out of the Gay Men's AIDS Prevention Task force in the early 90's, Gay City has been the product of collaboration between public health agencies and community activists. Our mission is to promote the health of gay and bisexual men and prevent HIV transmission by building community, fostering communication, and nurturing self-esteem.

Gay City is regarded nationally and internationally as a leader in prevention messaging and programming that is frank, bold, and reflective of contemporary gay culture. Blending community development, grassroots organizing, health education and advocacy with direct services, we have created programming that engages the community and empowers gay and bisexual men, including trans guys, to invest in being healthy.

Our success is born out of taking realistic approaches to health issues, and allowing members of our community to provide direction on each initiative. This approach is designed to result in sustainable and long-term change, and is based in behavioral theories of adult learning, diffusion of innovation, risk education, social marketing and empowerment.

To learn more about Gay City Health Project, please visit gaycity.org

PROGRAM HIGHLIGHTS

HIV/STD Testing and Counseling Gay City is the leading community-based provider of free, anonymous HIV/STD testing and free Hepatitis A & B vaccinations in King County. Since the opening of our Wellness Center in 2004, we have provided nearly 15,000 HIV tests, doubling the number of clients testing for HIV with us between 2004 and 2009. In 2010, we provided more than 2,300 HIV tests, reaching a record number of gay, bi and trans men who have sex with men, reaching a broad range of high-risk, hard-to-reach populations. Of our testing clients, 10% are first time testers, 40% are men of color, 41% are age 30 or under, and more than one-third do not have health insurance. Gay City identified 31% more new HIV infections in 2010 than in 2009. We've made a real difference in our community by being able to connect these men to the resources that they will need to stay healthy and a community they will need to gain support.

Gay City University is an annual daylong, peer led educational event that provides opportunities to share with and learn from their gay, bi, and trans male peers and allies. A broad range of classes is offered on subjects including health, finances, relationships, sexuality, queer history and a variety of recreational activities. In an internet connected and increasingly impersonal world,

Gay City University provides a much needed opportunity for real-time, personal, face-to-face interaction. It's also our longest running program. Queerituality is Gay City's monthly reading and discussion group for gay, bi, and trans men. It is focused on exploring our distinct spiritual experience, heritage, and gifts as queer men. Dozens of men meet regularly each month for reading, conversation, films, and outings around the growth of their queer spirituality.

Gay City Arts: We are a proud supporter of queer and queer-friendly arts, and include a variety of artistic programming as part our mission. In 2010, we published the 3rd volume of our Gay City Anthologies, a creative forum for previously unpublished comic art, fiction, poetry, and photography. We also presented the Seattle premiere of The Infection Monologues, a touching, humorous, and thought provoking performance that challenges the way we think about the contemporary experience of men living with HIV.

Gay City Sports: Organized athletics help to improve overall health on many levels: physical, mental, and social. Fortunately, the Seattle area has a vibrant LGBT sports community. Gay City adds to the mix with Team Gay City, our annual Seattle to Portland Classic bicycle team, and the Seattle SNAP, a Gay City sponsored sober ECSA softball team.

LGBT Resource and Referral Line: Part of building a healthy community is connecting LGBT people to the incredible resources available in Seattle and beyond. By managing Seattle's LGBT Resource and Referral Line, Gay City was able to provide more than 1,800 referrals last year to clients seeking access to community resources.

Gay City LGBT Library: In 2009, Gay City Health Project began to house and staff the LGBT Library after the closing of the Seattle LGBT Community Center. Last year the Gay City LGBT Library grew to a collection of over 2,200 volumes covering a wide range of LGBT topics. Staffed by volunteers, the Gay City LGBT library is a valuable community resource. Community members donate books, CDs and DVDs that can all be checked out for free.

Tobactivism: In 2010, we continued to act on our sense of social justice through our role as the Washington State contractor charged with addressing tobacco-related health disparities among LGBT individuals. We also continued provide innovative community leadership by leveraging the power of grant funding to take on the role of Presenting Sponsor at the 2011 Seattle Pride Fest celebration, allowing us to work with businesses and organizations that serve our community to develop policies for assisting their LGBT employees who wish to reduce or stop their tobacco use.

HOW YOU CAN HELP

Gay City Health Project was founded in response to the needs of the community. As we continue to to grow and change based on those changing needs, our commitment to our community remains as strong as ever. We recognize that our community's health is dependent upon the health of the broader community at large. We also recognize that our success in meeting those needs depends on your support. The success of our programs and services comes from the incredible support that we receive from volunteers, donors, local businesses and partnering organizations.

Despite the economic uncertainty that continues to affect us all, Gay City has continued to provide a variety of much needed programs and services to gay men and the LGBT community as a whole. While budgets and services continue to be reduced or eliminated entirely, the needs of the gay community – our community, your community – continue to grow. Your donations ensure that everyone seeking help and support from Gay City can receive it.

You have the power to make an impact. You have the ability to influence the health and future of the gay community by making a contribution to Gay City Health Project.

You can donate online at gaycity.org/donate, or send your tax-deductible contribution to:

Gay City Health Project
511 E Pike Street
Seattle, WA 98122

Epilogue

Vincent Kovar

When I created this series of anthologies I was already looking forward and sub-titled the first book, *volume one* in anticipation of those to come. Now, five years and four books later, it's time for a look back.

As a community and a nation, we've come a long way during this period. Don't ask-Don't Tell has been consigned to the dustbin of history. Same-sex marriage has been legalized in several states and the so-called Defense of Marriage Act has been labelled indefensible by the US Justice Department.

It's been a time of reviewing our values and for taking a second glance at a lot of things. But, we aren't only looking for what's different. I think we're also looking around to see what's still familiar. Yes, the world is a different place and maybe we're even different people but there's still a home for our familiar stories.

The contributors to this volume venture out into this new-old, familiar-strange territory. They explore the myths, satires, allegories, fables and fiction that once defined who we were and they've come back with fresh, new interpretations that illuminate who we've become.

The stories in this book range across continents, time-periods and the topography of the imagination. They take a trip down the Mississippi, dash through ancient Greece, do a low-flyby over Great Britain, stop off at the doctor's office and more, more, more.

These subtle (and often not-so-subtle) shifts in the literary landscape give us, the readers, the thrill of seeing familiar characters experiencing changes no less dramatic than the ones we've undergone.

They're finding their voice, finding love, finding themselves; often for the first time ever. What they get to keep is another question. Like Californians facing Proposition 8, not all of the characters in our tales find success easy to hold onto. Sometimes life can feel like we're taking one step forward and two steps back. But perhaps that's not so bad. True success sometimes takes the long way around. Maybe we've dropped magic keys or encoded clues along the way. Maybe there's even shortcuts and secret passages hidden behind us. If so, looking backwards is worth a second glance.

Vincent Kovar

is a college professor, journalist, playwright, editor living in Seattle, WA. His fiction has recently appeared in *A Touch of Lavender: Queering Sherlock Holmes* (ed. Joseph R.G. De Marco) while future pieces will be published in *A Touch of the Sea* (ed. Stever Berman) and *Tales of the New Mexican Mythos: Weird Fiction from the Land of Enchantment* (ed. Paul C. Bustamonte). He'd like to once again thank the givers of grants, the sponsors, our friends and everybody at Gay City Health Project for making this anthology series possible.

Made in the USA
Charleston, SC
14 January 2012